WOMEN
OF THE
FOREST

BY
LINDA J. ORMSON

To Lynn:

"In celebration of great service"

Warm blessings

Linda J. Ormson

WARM THOUGHTS PUBLISHING
1996

ISBN 0-9693900-1-7

Canadian Cataloguing in Publication Data

Ormson, Linda J. (Linda Joan), 1953-
Women of the Forest

Includes bibliographical references.
ISBN 0-9693900-1-7

1. Women—Health and hygiene. I Title.
RA564.85O76 1996   613'.04244   C96-910135-X

Editor: Maureen McManus

Cover Design: Brad Hendricks

Previous books by the author: SOCKS… and other warm thoughts.

Orders and Inquiries to:
Warm Thoughts Publishing
112 Woodmont Drive S.W.
Calgary, Alberta, Canada
T2W 4M3
Fax: 238-0482

Printed in Canada by Emerson Clarke Printing

Dedicated in memory of my
pioneer grandparents:
Barbara & Frank Bengert
Rachel & Jeremiah Leavitt

And especially to my parents:
Elda & Ernest Bengert

Thank you for your love and support;
for teaching me the values of hard work,
and the benefits of carrying
a positive attitude.

cknowledgements

When one throws a pebble into a pond, it creates a ripple that touches every point in the water. People are my ripples. Each person who has touched my life, has in some way changed who I am. I would like to acknowledge a few of the many ripples, who give me energy and have helped me to be a better human being.

Thank you to my Christian Women's Fellowship group, of Campbell-Stone United Church. You are all wonderful gifts who have given me love, support, friendship and prayers.

To Calgary Women's Network… a wonderful group of women who support other women in business.

Gratitude to my Registered Nurse colleagues and friends who read and gave input into the manuscript of Women of the Forest. Thanks to: Anne Welsh-Baskett, Lee Wallace, Lorraine Sinclair, Cynthia Mills, Dianne Fownes, Marilyn Hannay and Barb Nobert.

To the women in my life who continue to inspire me: Anne Cunningham, Karen Hacking, Marlene Hamilton, Susan Cross, Simone De Cnodder and Aline Roberts.

Special thanks to Joy Fraser, MN, RN, Ph.D (student), Associate Professor from Athabasca University and Cathy Connors RN, MN, from the Breast Health Program, Grace Women's Health Centre, Calgary.

To "a gifted woman of thought," my editor Maureen McManus for her enthusiasm, keen eye and support throughout this project.

To my children Jonathan and Leah for their daily deposit of hugs.

And finally to Jackson, my life-partner and friend, who gives me constant support. Thanks for sharing all the laughter and tears… it's all been good!

Linda

TABLE OF CONTENTS

 n Invitation

I would like to invite you on a journey into a mythical forest. This is an adventure of self-discovery written for and about women. Travel with four middle-aged women as they hike west of Calgary. You will learn right along with them about the unique trees and animals of this special forest. And most importantly, you will learn about six women's health and wellness issues as Barb, Sue, Liz and Kim share their stories. These women, like you and the forest, have cycles and seasons. Come along, make a friend and discover something about yourself.

HAPTER ONE

Barb finished packing her lettuce and tomato sandwich into her backpack and closed it with the distinct sound of the zip! It was Wednesday morning, a morning she had looked forward to all week. Her other women friends would be meeting her at the birch grove at the edge of the forest and she would have to hurry in order to make the 30-minute drive west of the city in time.

From the front hallway she grabbed her husband's green cable knit sweater. It was a perfect weight for cool Fall mornings such as this. The sweater still smelled of him and as she pulled it on over her shoulders, she was warmed and aroused by its scent. As her face poked through the opening, her eyes focused on the family portrait sitting on the Victorian table near the front door. The portrait, taken only one year ago, displayed two young men, her sons, both in their early twenties. They had her olive skin and dark eyes. Barb's father was a native West Indian from Trinidad and her mother was British. Phillip, her husband, wore the familiar sweater in the picture. A gentle, but strong, loving man, he had been taken over and consumed by cancer just six months ago.

Moments passed until the chime from the hallway clock broke her solitary thoughts. It was 8:00 a.m. Barb drew in a deep breath, then let it slowly ease out of her, as a tire would when deflating. The portrait made her both happy and sad at the same time. Taking her final look at it, she found herself reaching for the front door, knowing that she must move on. A tear had settled on the bottom edge of her left eyelid and soon it cascaded down her cheek onto the green cable knit sweater. She stepped outside, pulled the door shut and locked it to keep contents and memories safe inside. The morning air was fresh and crisp, renewing Barb's pleasant thoughts of her female companions. As she pulled out of the driveway, thoughts of Phillip and loneliness soon vanished into the Fall air.

The sun was behind her as she headed west along the Trans-Canada Highway. It was early September and a few trees had been sprinkled with gold leaves to catch the morning sun. The motor of her Toyota hummed along and she soon found herself singing to one of The Rankin Family's new Gaelic tunes on the radio. Time sped by, as did the kilometres. Soon, she was pulling into the parking lot at the edge of the forest.

Barb knew that Liz and Sue already had arrived when she saw the familiar maroon mini-van, but its occupants were absent. The two women were just around a bend near their favourite meeting place… the birch grove. Barb was pleased to see her two new friends give a friendly wave from the old tree stump where they sat. They loved nature as much as she did.

"Hi, you two," said Barb, as she walked along the well-worn dirt path.

"Good to see you, Barb," said Sue, who wrapped a warm embrace around her tawny-coloured friend. Barb returned the gift with a healthy squeeze of her own.

"Hey," declared Liz, "can I get in on some of those warm fuzzies too?" Liz joined in to make a triad of hugs. "Friends," contemplated Barb, "where would one be without friends?"

After Phillip's death, she knew that she needed to get out and meet some new people. Phillip had always been the social one of the pair, making friends easily and Phillip was her best friend. Barb was a 53-year-old, part-time nurse whose life had revolved around Phillip. She never thought that one day she would be alone without him or his friends. After his death, Barb found herself lonely and isolated. Then in July, while sitting in her peaceful backyard garden, she made a decision about her life. She decided to become more proactive about making new friends... she had a plan! Barb's love of the outdoors would become the common link to gather some women together. They would meet weekly for a day of hiking and companionship. Barb knew just the place. A large virgin forest lay west of the city with hiking trails, rivers and small lakes. The lush, green forest was also filled with wildlife, flowers and trees of all kinds from across Canada.

In the two days that followed, Barb placed posters at local stores and strip malls in the neighbourhood. Barb also ran a small ad in the community newsletter. Within six days, she was talking to her first interested caller. Sue was a 45-year-old mother of three teenage girls, who had stayed home to care for her family's needs. Even though Sue had been busy raising her girls, she still found time to work out at the fitness centre three times a week. Her muscular figure was attractive for her 5 foot 6 inch height and was complimented by her short, dark brown hair, sprinkled with grey. Sue's husband had started working long hours because of a building boom in the city and her teenagers had become more independent. Sue soon became bored staying at home. She was friendly and outgoing, so the job at the local coffee bar making cappuccinos and listening to people's problems met most of her care-giving needs. However, a gap remained... until she saw Barb's poster at the mall where she worked. Sue called Barb that night.

Liz was Barb's next caller. When the 51-year-old was not in front of her grade five class, she was busy caring for her 82-year-old mother who lived with her. The professional teacher had never married. She was content with her busy, but fulfilling, life. Her auburn hair and green eyes suited her round face and she joked about her extra weight being her life-long companion. However, this past spring Liz found herself with a rigorous schedule. Teaching was becoming more challenging with all the education cutbacks and her frail mother had several boughts of flu. Liz was eating more fast and high-fat snack foods due to lack of time to cook a nourishing meal. By June, Liz's health had become a major concern: her weight, along with her blood pressure was up; and then there was the lump she had found while practising Breast Self-Examination. In early August, she had already decided to reduce her teaching days to four per week and start having the Victorian Order of Nurses provide daily home nursing care for her mother. She had realized that her doctor's warning about lifestyle choices could no longer go unheeded. She wanted to take better control of her life. Answering Barb's ad in the community newsletter was going to be the catalyst to help her do just that!

Barb broke off from the triad's embrace first and asked, "Is Kim here yet?"

"No, not yet," responded Sue, "but she'll be along. She is trying out another new babysitter today, so she may be a few minutes late." Sue turned to Liz and commented further, "I'm sure glad my babysitting days are over, although having three teenagers is no piece of cake!" She rolled her eyes upward and smiled.

"How are all your girls doing in school this Fall, Sue?" questioned Liz.

"Heaven only knows some days," replied Sue. "They dash in and out like cars through a wash and if one is not on the phone, the other two want to use it. Our house is like rush-hour on the Deerfoot Trail... it's mayhem." Sue gave a big sigh, smiled at Liz and said further, "Actually, they are pretty normal and settling in at their schools just fine." Barb gave Sue a knowing smile as she recalled her boys at the same age.

"Sounds like you have your hands full, Sue," commented Liz, "I'm glad my involvement with children ends in the classroom each day; I'm not sure if I could handle them full-time like you two."

"Oh sure you could," said Sue, "the trick is to just do what you have to do, not think too far ahead and send everyone out with a hug each day. It's the thinking about something that usually is overwhelming and exhausts us out before we even begin."

"That's certainly true," commented Barb, "every day, sometimes every moment, has its challenges." All three women nodded their heads, affirming the statement that now hung in the air before them, thinking of their own challenges that lay ahead.

The sound of a car horn aroused them from their thoughts. "Hi, everyone," called Kim, while locking the door of her red Saturn. "Sorry I'm late. I thought Kyle would never stop crying at the new sitter. It's days like these I wonder why we decided on children so late in life. At 41, I should be hanging around Club Med, not hanging out diapers!"

"Don't be silly Kim," said Sue, "you and Rob are great parents. Look at all the quality time you spend with your 18-month-old. I had my girls in my early 20s, you know... bang, bang and finally Bang! I never had five minutes to myself, I was always rushing somewhere... we never seemed to have good quality time." As Kim looked at Sue, she thought she seemed tired just remembering those days and was pleased that Kyle was the only child she planned to have.

"Cheer up Sue," announced Kim, "today is Wednesday and we are about to embark on another day of adventure in Mother Nature's own."

Barb smiled at Kim's enthusiasm and recalled when Kim first called her. Kim was 12 years younger than her and a breath of fresh air in Barb's stale world. Kim's parents came from Hong Kong to Canada when Kim was seven. The spunky new Canadian followed her parents' hard-working ethics and studied diligently at school. She graduated from the Faculty of Law with honours and, shortly after, married another Hong Kong immigrant who was a talented engineer. The couple spent the next fifteen years working on their careers without regret. Then one day they both suddenly realized that they wanted a family. Their new son was a real joy to them but also a real handful. Kim was working full-time in a large law firm, as well as being a mother and wife. She needed to have some quality time of her own. Finding Barb's poster at the local grocery store was more than luck... it was a gift! Kim rescheduled her work-week to keep Wednesdays free and had two alternate babysitters lined up to care for Kyle. Now Kim looked forward to joining her new women friends for a day of fellowship, fun and fresh air.

At 8:45 a.m., the women strapped their day packs on and tightened their footwear. "What a unique group of women I have gathered," thought Barb, as she adjusted the backpack over her green sweater. These women of the forest had come together in early August to learn weekly about the forest and themselves. Each leaf and tree they touched became a gift and strengthened their need to know and learn more from each other. As if in concert, the four women announced, "Everyone ready." Smiles and laughter followed.

"I take that as a 'yes'," giggled Barb, "whose turn to lead?"

"I think it's mine," called out Sue, "I've never been much of a leader in life, but how difficult can this be with you assertive women pushing me from behind?"

"I'm right behind you, Sue," said Kim, giving an encouraging smile. "Today we follow Sue!"

The birch grove was a kilometre wide and stood as the doorway to the forest. Following Sue, the women walked farther into the birch grove, heading west until they reached the thick, lush green pines. This forest was unique among all others, as it lay at the footsteps of the Canadian Rockies. Here, all kinds of trees grew in abundance. Trees normally found in southern Ontario, like maple and oak also grew here, as did elders from British Columbia and poplars, willow and pines. With each day trip the women took through the forest, they were awed by its unique beauty.

"It's like walking across Canada," said Kim, using her eyes as a camera lens. Sue, only six paces ahead of her, was announcing to the birds flying above the trees, "wonderful, wonderful!"

The women of the forest wandered on. Every now and then, one of them would stop and discover something unusual, halting the other three. No one minded. In fact, that was the way they all wanted it... all to learn, all to enjoy. Sue led them into a small clearing, where they were surrounded by small birds that scurried about in the air and amongst the trees.

"What kind of birds are those?" asked Liz.

Kim was the first to respond, "I think they are Black-capped Chickadees. They usually fly in a flock of dozens of birds, flitting between the trees and shrubs, searching for insects and berries. They keep an eye on each other, so if one finds a tidbit, its fellow-flyers enthusiastically carry on the search for more."

"Gosh, that sounds like us," announced Sue. "We look out for each other and when one of us finds something interesting, we all appear at the finder's side like jam on peanut butter!" Dozens of the little flyers suddenly disappeared at the sound of the four's laughter over the analogy.

After Barb's final giggle, she gestured to Sue and then proclaimed, "Hey, Ms. Leader of the Peanut-Butter-and-Jam Troop, since you are the one who brought up the subject of food, it's nearly 12:30. Let's call a halt right here." A large grin appeared on Sue's face to second the motion.

"Ooh," said Kim, as she stretched her arms up as far as they could go, "I'm ready for a break."

"Me too," said Liz, as she reached into her pack for a cold pop. After taking a long, well-needed gulp of cold refreshment, she stretched out on the ground and stared up at the sky. "What a great morning," said Liz, "we discovered at least five different trees and shrubs, birds of all colours and I can't believe that bed of moss growing over those large rocks near the Douglas Fir trees."

"It's really spectacular," confirmed Kim. "Two months ago, I was reading about this forest in my *Canadian Geographic* and for the past four weeks I have been taking it in step-by-step." Kim's eyes scanned the green veil of shrubs and trees that surrounded them.

"I'm glad you think so too," said Barb, as she opened her bottle of Evian water. "I always wanted to come back here and explore, but needed to have companions to share it with. I felt it would be a wonderful place to bond with nature and learn about myself at the same time."

"We're glad you did," responded Sue, giving Barb a warm hug to thank her for all her efforts.

"Say Sue," asked Liz, as she rose back into a sitting position, "what are those bushes over there by the creek?"

Sue gave Barb a final squeeze, then walked over to inspect another new find. "Oh, they're chokecherry bushes. They usually ripen by the end of August, but these are all dried up now. I've made jelly and pancake syrup from the berries for years. The native Canadians used them for making pemmican. They would pound the berries into a mash, then pound the mash into the meat before drying. It helped to preserve the meat."

Sue moved away from the chokecherry bushes and headed for her backpack. "Speaking of pemmican," said Barb, "my lettuce and tomato sandwich is looking pretty good right now." As Barb reached for her sandwich and took a hearty bite, Liz munched on a large red apple. The sound of the Macintosh broke the rustling of plastic wrap from Sue's whole-wheat bagel.

"Oh sorry," mumbled Liz with a mouthful of apple, her hand now covering her mouth as she chewed. Liz's companions all smiled at their friend who was still self-conscious of her size. After adjusting a portion of apple into the other cheek, Liz said, "This weekly hiking and you women have been a real positive influence on me, I lost another pound this week."

"That's terrific, Liz!" said Barb, giving her friend encouragement, "when you change your dietary habits and increase your activity levels, you'll slowly start to lose weight and that's the best way to keep it off."

After swallowing the B.C. fruit, Liz spoke. "I should have paid more attention to *Canada's Food Guide to Healthy Eating* years ago, instead of all those fad food diets. I dieted my way up to 195 pounds! Yo-yo dieting, I think they call it."

"That's right Liz," said Sue, "I had a friend who was always on a diet of one kind or another. She would diet for two weeks and lose a little weight, only to gain it back and more the moment she went off it."

The women continued to eat for a few minutes without speaking, then after Liz finished her drink she began again. "By June I had gained so much weight that I almost missed feeling that lump in my right breast. I'm quite heavy there anyway," she said, looking down at both of her breasts. Returning her gaze to her friends, she said, "Thank heavens for Breast Self-Exam!"

Barb then asked Liz, "Have you always practised BSE, Liz?"

Liz became more alert after the question and answered, "Oh yes, it's one of my good health habits that I do practise."

Liz moved to sit on an old tree stump to get more comfortable and then asked her companions, "How about you gals?" Liz looked from one woman to the next and was met with an uncomfortable silence. "You're all kidding, right!" exclaimed Liz looking over to Barb. "Barb, you're a nurse, surely you practise BSE!"

"Well, actually," Barb's voice was slow and hesitant, "only now and again."

Sue then added, "I guess I'm like many women; I'm not confident what I'm feeling for because I've never been taught. I remember feeling so embarrassed the first time I practised BSE."

"Those are valid reasons why many women do not practice BSE," said Liz, as she turned to Sue. "I remember feeling uneasy the first time too Sue, but since there is a history of breast cancer in my family and I've never had children and I eat a high-fat diet, I'm at a greater risk than other women. BSE is one way a woman can be aware of her body's changes. You're in charge, so to speak." Liz continued, "I was taught by the health clinic's nurse seven years ago and have practised monthly ever since."

"But what are you actually feeling for," asked Sue, "my breasts are so lumpy. Is that normal?"

"Most breast tissue is lumpy," responded Liz, "similar to cottage cheese or tapioca. Some women have more lumpiness than others and often one breast has more lumpiness than the other one," Liz said assuringly, "but it's normal!" Liz now stood as she would when lecturing her grade five class on an important issue and continued. "What you are actually feeling for is a change in the lumpiness, something different, like a three-dimensional pebble in your breast."

Kim, who had been sitting back listening carefully to every word her friends spoke, looked at Liz and then asked, "So, is that what you found Liz?"

"Yes, Kim. You see after practising BSE for so many years, I have come to know my breasts pretty well. What I found was a change from normal and that's all doctors expect from you... just to know when there is something different and to go and have it checked out." Liz sat again, then continued, "What I had in my right breast was a lumpy area which the doctors removed by surgical biopsy. Breast tissue changes as we age and I had a small area where there was a fibrocystic change. It was not cancer, but if it had been and I had not practised BSE, I could have put my life in danger."

The other three women took deep breaths of the fresh pine-scented air, as if to clear the negative image of losing their new friend.

"I've heard and read about BSE," said Kim, "but I thought only women in their forties and fifties... you know around menopause... were to practise it."

"Actually," said Barb, "I was reading in a nursing journal, that health practicioners suggest women in their early twenties start BSE, not because they are at particular risk, but to get comfortable with the habit and their normal breast texture."

"That's an excellent idea," stated Liz "and the best time to practice it is about seven to fourteen days into your menstrual cycle. Some women experience breast swelling and tenderness premenstrually, so the best time is after your period. Women who are post-menopausal," continued Liz, "should pick a date and use the calendar as a reminder." As Liz said her final words, she looked over at Barb to see a very sad expression etched on her face. "What is it Barb?" asked Liz in a caring voice.

Barb looked from one woman to the other before she spoke, "I seem to put off BSE month after month. I guess I'm afraid of what I might find... like Phillip's cancer." Before she took her next breath, she was surrounded by three women who wanted to support her.

Kim kneeled directly in front of her, touched her cheek softly and said, "But if most of the breasts' changes are a normal part of aging, women like us should move beyond fear and take more control of our bodies."

Barb gave her Oriental friend a gentle smile and said, "I know you are right, Kim, but sometimes it's hard to do just the same."

As the women remained huddled around Barb, Sue commented, "I agree with Kim. Using a positive health practice such as Breast Self-Exam is a proactive choice that could save our lives. Look at all the things women spend time and money on to look and feel their best, you know like, hair, nails, exercise, dental appointments... BSE should become part of our routine."

"And I use my monthly agenda book to mark in all my scheduled exercise workouts," said Kim, the new mother committed to returning to her size eight. "I might as well mark the calendar to practice BSE too. Mind you, I don't know how to do it," said Kim, pleading for help from her older friends.

"I picked up a brochure from the drug store a couple of months back," said Sue, "I'm sure it's still in my desk drawer where I left it. Maybe it's time to dig it out and take a serious look at BSE; after all, women are a precious resource!"

"Yes we are," said Barb, who had remained quiet for several minutes, "and having women friends like all of you confirms it." The warm, genuine smile on Barb's face gave a clear message to her walking companions.

From the west, sunrays filtered through the treetops to signal the passing of time. Each woman slowly started to gather her daypack and prepare to return to the birch grove. Liz watched her friends for a moment as boot laces were tightened and packs adjusted. Then, in a slightly emotional voice, she spoke to all of them, "I'm so proud to know all of you!" Heads turned upward to see who had gifted them with such caring words.

All three women smiled warmly as Barb responded, "That goes double for you, Liz. This forest brings out the best in all of us."

"We're all seeking quality time to bring out the best in ourselves," said Sue, as she took up her position in front of the group.

Liz took up the position behind Sue and said, "That's what I like so much about all of you, you're willing to learn new things and change old habits for the betterment of yourself and others you meet. And Breast Self-Exam is all about just that... health enhancement!"

Liz's words were like a final paragraph in the chapter of their day. The women then began to follow Sue on their return journey east along the path. Very few words were spoken on their way back to the birch grove. It was a peaceful way to end a day of adventure and self-discovery. As Sue and Liz placed their daypacks into the mini-van, Kim was already driving out of the parking lot waving as she drove. Barb's Toyota was warm inside, so she opened the windows to capture some of nature's late afternoon scent. She waved at Sue and Liz as they drove away. Several minutes passed before she rolled up the windows and started the car.

It was nearly 4:00 p.m. and Barb's sons would be home from university and starting dinner for the three of them. Barb's mind continued to focus on the conversation that had occurred in the forest. As a Registered Nurse, Barb had always presented health promotion ideas to her clients, so why was it so difficult for her to practise what she preached? "Sue was right," she thought, "women need to be in control of their bodies and their health. My fear of illness has kept me from doing that." Just then the sun peeked out from a passing cloud and brightly illuminated the car. "I must also come out from behind a cloud," thought Barb, "I must move on." The image of the sun and the cloud was a positive affirmation for Barb, which left a peaceful smile on her face as she drove away from the forest.

BSE For Every Woman: A New Approach to Breast Self-Examination

Printed with permission from The Canadian Cancer Society

1. Visual Check

a. Stand in front of a mirror and look at your breasts carefully — first face forward and then turn slowly side to side.

b. Lift your arms above your head and behind your ears. If you have pendulous breasts you may need to lift them up to see the lower halves.

c. Lower your hands part-way and squeeze your palms together.

Look for: overall changes in shape, size, or contour. Obvious lumps, dimpling, flattening, reddening. Nipple flattening, indrawing, or pointing in a new direction. Also look for sores or rashes.

Continued on page 14

2. Hand Check — Standing

Use the opposite hand for each breast.

a. circular motion

a. Use a flat hand. Bend your wrist, not your fingers to go over curves. Apply moderate pressure and keep constant contact with your skin.

flat hand,
constant contact,
correct pressure

b. Move back and forth across the breast in a straight line pattern, making constant small circles. Slide your hand down one finger width for each pass. Cover the full area indicated.

not like this

c. Check the area under your arm. Relax your arm, place your hand under it, making the same small circular movements as before.

What are you checking for? If you feel anything that is a different texture or movement than what you've felt before — that's the time to consult your doctor. Remember that it may be normal for your breasts to be lumpy — you're checking for something that wasn't there last month.

b.

c.

3. Hand Check — Lying Down

In the last step of BSE, lie down on a firm surface. Use exactly the same steps used when standing. It is not necessary to check your underarm while lying down.

Notes

_____

_____

_____

_____

_____

_____

_____

_____

_____

CHAPTER TWO

The coffee shop where Sue worked had been busy all day. The half-price sale had filled the mall with people, who gathered for a cup of coffee, to rest and talk about their purchases. As Sue began to tidy up in preparation to close the shop, she smiled at the thought of tomorrow... yes Wednesday... how she loved her Wednesdays! Sue had arranged to pick up her friends at the mall parking lot and all drive out together. But for now, she was tired and her feet ached from standing a good part of the day. Sue poured the last of the stale coffee down the sink and wiped the counter-tops. She looked forward to going home and having a hot, steamy bath. Since Sue worked until 6:00 p.m. every Tuesday night, her girls normally fixed their own supper. "Teens seem to eat the moment they walk in the door," she thought; "they are always hungry and on the go." Now that they were older, Sue was pleased that she no longer had to make them dinner every night. She was slowly gaining some time back for herself. After locking up the shop, she stopped at the small deli on her way out of the mall and bought a salmon sandwich. It was dark outside and the Fall air was crisp, as she walked to her mini-van. "Where did the Summer go?" she thought. "The seasons seem to move faster each year." There were only a few cars left in the parking lot when she pulled away... a true sign that the day was over for everyone.

On Sue's drive home, no other thoughts seemed to register, until she pulled into the familiar driveway. All the house lights were on... a welcome sign at the end of the day. Her husband's car was not in its parking space next to hers. He was a man passionate about his work... architecture... and spent long hours over his blueprints. Because of the recent building boom in the city, he worked very hard and only came home when he was too exhausted to work any longer. "I miss him," Sue thought, as she stared at the oil patch on the driveway, which normally was hidden by his parked car. "Maybe he won't have to work too late tonight," her thoughts continued, "and we can have a nightcap together." Sue crossed her fingers, thinking about her husband of twenty years and stepped out of the van.

After entering the home, Sue tossed her coat over the railing near the entrance and headed for the kitchen. There, she poured a healthy glass of cold, skimmed milk, unwrapped her sandwich and began to eat her evening meal. She could hear the TV, a radio and someone having a telephone conversation, all at the same time and wondered how homework could ever be accomplished with all the distractions. Her daughters' ages were 17, 15 and 13. "Can I survive?" wondered Sue, as she finished drinking her milk. She was a supportive mother, who always made time for each daughter's needs. However, at times she wondered about meeting some of her own needs! With that thought, Sue headed to the bathroom to draw a hot bath. Soon she found herself soaking in a pool of steamy, rose-scented water, which seemed to release the tired feeling from her body. The relaxing, misty moment was interrupted as her youngest daughter, Dawn, flung open the bathroom door with no notice.

"Oh, hi Mom," said Dawn, "how was your day?" The cool air stung Sue's exposed skin, so she quickly sunk deeper into the water to capture more heat.

"Busy," stated the tired mother of three, "and please close the door."

"Sure... sorry Mom," said Dawn, "I heard you come in earlier and wanted to let you know that Grandma called. She wants you to call her back." With that comment, Dawn rushed out of the bathroom to get a ringing phone and flung the bathroom door shut. Sue sighed, sunk even deeper into the tub and wondered when she would ever get a moment's peace.

Later in the evening, Sue returned her mother's telephone call. Sue's mother was a 75-year-old widow, recuperating from two fractured ribs. She had developed a bad cold and broke the ribs after a coughing spell last month. Sue's mother had become quite frail since fracturing her right wrist and having three vertebra collapse earlier in the year. Osteoporosis was the silent culprit, which had reduced her mother's bone mass and made her susceptible to more falls. Sue worried about her mother constantly and long after the telephone conversation ended, Sue continued to think about her mom.

By 8:45 the next morning, all four women had arrived at the edge of the forest in Sue's van. It had been fun to meet at the mall, get coffees to go and visit with each other on the drive west of the city. Once out of the van, the women began their routine preparation of lacing up boots and adjusting day-packs, before they started their hike. On this crisp, Fall morning, Liz led the way to the southwest corner of the forest, where a grove of maple trees grew. "I can't wait to see those bright red and orange leaves," said an excited Kim.

"Me, too," commented Liz, "I've never been out to Ontario or Quebec where they grow so abundantly."

After following the hour-long trail, which wandered by a small stream, the vibrant colours of the maples did not disappoint any of the women. Their path ended near a clearing in the woods, where the maples surrounded and guarded the perimeter of the small meadow.

"This is so... so... Canadian!" exclaimed Sue, as she took in the magnificent colours, like a breath of fresh air.

Liz responded to Sue's remark, "You're right, Sue, the maple leaf has been considered an appropriate emblem for Canada for a long time, thanks to all the maple trees that grow in our country." Liz set down her pack and continued to speak. "I taught my grade five class a unit on this topic last Fall. Maple leaves were first used in coats of arms granted to Ontario and Quebec in 1868 and then on the

Canadian Coat of Arms in 1921. The maple leaf was used on regimental badges for our soldiers in World War I and II and was confirmed as a national symbol in 1965, with the proclamation of the national flag." Liz reached up to gently touch the tip of a maple leaf hanging down from the tree near her and then added, "I remember seeing pictures of my dad wearing his uniform in the Second World War. The maple leaf emblem stood out on the sleeve of his tunic, as if to tell the world how proud he was to be Canadian."

Kim, who was kneeling next to Liz, was busy picking up some of the undamaged fallen leaves. "I'm taking a few of these leaves home to show Rob," stated Kim, then continued, "when we took classes on becoming Canadian citizens, we learned how maple syrup is made, but I've never seen a real maple tree before." As Kim looked from leaf to leaf, she spotted a red one, which was larger than her hand and carefully picked it up. She held the leaf up to the light… as if to add a sunbeam's blessing to it, before storing it carefully in her pack.

Sue moved over to where Kim and Liz were standing. She reached out and touched the bark of the large tree shading the path which had led them here. Her fingers massaged each crack and crevice, enjoying the feel of the rough, yet strong texture. Sue raised her eyes to meet both her friends and added her own piece of information about the beautiful tree. "An Iroquois legend tells about piercing the bark of a maple tree in early Spring and using the syrup, called 'sweet water', to cook venison. French settlers," she added, "probably learned from the natives how to tap the trees to obtain the sap."

"I think the Ojibwa called the sugaring-off period, 'the sugar month'," commented Liz, as she touched the tree bark next to Sue's still-caressing hand.

Kim had been listening to every word her friends spoke about the magnificent tree. She was always wanting to learn more about Canada, its people and the gifts from nature. Kim thought a moment before speaking to her friends, "Nature gives this land and its people so very much. It's too bad we take it with such greed and rarely, if ever, return anything to Mother Earth!" The three women stood silent, contemplating the truth in what Kim had said and perhaps thinking of how they had also taken from the earth. They stood dwarfed in fragile beauty.

The air was warming quickly, as the sun stretched over the crimson leaves to touch each woman with a hint of flame. The crunching of leaves underfoot drew them back from their personal thoughts. Barb had wandered off to the nearby stream to seek out her own virgin territory. She enjoyed her friends immensely, but after a long hike, she always wanted a silent cleansing of her spirit near the water. The other women respected her few minutes of solitude and knew that she would join them shortly. Sometimes Barb would hum a peaceful tune or pray. Today she just sat and listened to the water as it danced over the rocks. As Barb left the stream, its sound was slowly muffled by her footsteps on the sun-dried leaves. When Barb reached the clearing, where she had left her friends ten minutes before, she found them frozen in place. They were like the trees they visited, touched with sunbeams and standing motionless... one with Mother Earth. Barb smiled at the picture before her for several moments. Her footsteps then broke the silence and her friends soon awoke from its spell. As Barb joined her walking companions, she spoke. "You three are really getting into this nature stuff. Are you gals OK?"

The women's posture was now more relaxed and they all smiled warmly at Barb. "We can't help it;" said Sue, "it's an addiction."

"It's even better than chocolate," stated Liz, grabbing her pack to search for a cold drink.

"What time is it anyway?" asked Sue, "it must be almost noon."

"Actually, it's only 11:15," answered Kim, looking at her watch.

"Well that's close enough for me," proclaimed Liz and started to unwrap a low-fat cheese sandwich.

Sue smiled at her friend, as she sat on a fresh bed of maple leaves. "Ah yes," announced Sue, "we go by nature's time!"

The Fall air, exercise and wonder of the forest had certainly stirred up the appetites of the women. Within minutes, they were all unpacking their lunches and drinks. After a few minutes, Barb asked,

"So what were you all standing so still for... did you see a deer or something?"

Sue swallowed a bite of her whole-wheat bagel and answered for her friends who were still chewing. "We were just thinking about what nature... you know... the trees, plants and animals give to us, and how little we give back in return."

"That's a pretty heavy topic," commented Barb, "no wonder you were all spellbound when I found you!"

Kim finished drinking her diet-pop and said, "Actually Barb, we started off by talking about how maple syrup comes from the sap of maple trees."

Barb nodded her head in response to Kim's comment, then added, "Last Fall, I worked relief on a cardiac unit at the hospital. They used maple syrup as a natural sweetener, rather than sugar or honey. Apparently maple syrup has a lot of trace minerals such as potassium, magnesium and especially calcium." She continued, "In fact, maple syrup has fifteen times the amount of calcium than in honey! My older sister has been on a salt-restricted diet for years, because of her high blood pressure. She uses maple syrup in her tea and coffee because it contains about one-tenth the sodium of honey."

"Calcium in maple syrup," proclaimed Liz, finishing a juicy pear, "who would have thought?"

Sue turned to Liz and commented, "Actually there are lots of foods that contain calcium, besides milk and dairy products. Since my mother was diagnosed with osteoporosis, I've become more aware of food sources that are high in calcium."

"How is your mother doing, Sue?" questioned Barb.

"She's healing very slowly," responded Sue. "This is her third session of broken bones this year!"

Kim, who was sitting next to Sue, thought that Sue looked quite discouraged when she spoke about her mother. As Kim gently touched Sue's shoulder, she asked, "What causes osteoporosis anyway? Is it because people don't drink enough milk?" Sue and the other women looked to Barb for some answers, because their friend was a Registered Nurse.

"Well," started Barb, "a woman's bone mass usually peaks at age 35. After that time, women tend to lose about 1% every year... 10% a decade. And by the time a woman reaches 65, she loses an additional 3%–4% a decade of bone mass. Barb then added, "Women over 35 years of age absorb calcium less easily. That's why children and especially teenage girls, should eat a diet rich in calcium... to lay down a dense bone framework that will carry them in later life."

"Since my mother was diagnosed with osteoporosis," stated Sue, "I've really encouraged my girls to drink as much skimmed milk as they can. My teens, having seen their grandmother's pain and loss of mobility, know how devastating this disease can be."

Liz, who had been sitting quietly, shifted her position on the dried leaves and commented, "Sounds like a good health practice for your girls, Sue! But how do you know if you have osteoporosis anyway?"

Barb once again answered, "It's usually discovered when an older person bends to lift an object and hears a snapping sound, followed by sudden pain in the lower back. Or, in the case of Sue's mother, when she coughed and broke two ribs."

Then Sue interrupted, "Or like when she fell and broke her wrist. Her bones are so brittle that any fall will likely result in a broken bone. Sometimes the bones just spontaneously break and cause a fall." Sue also decided to change her position and crossed her legs in a lotus fashion, like a sitting Buddha. She then looked back at her friends and continued, "I've seen my mother's x-rays. The inside of her bones look like a broken spider's web... with large holes!"

"You know," interrupted Liz, "my grandmother was once a tall woman. I remember when she got older, she became bent over and shorter than me... I think it was called 'Dowager's Hump'... was that osteoporosis Barb?"

"Very likely, Liz," answered, Barb. "In advanced osteoporosis, the spine becomes compressed and collapses, resulting in deformity, where a person becomes severely humped forward. This reduces height and often creates severe back pain."

"Does this only happen to women?" asked Kim, who had a serious look on her face when she asked the question.

"Oh, no," answered Barb, "men too, but women are at greater risk because they are often smaller boned to begin with. Young girls, and many women, are especially weight conscious and they often skip the calcium products which help make our bones healthy and strong. Estrogen is also believed to help reduce osteoporosis by keeping our bones dense. After menopause, women's estrogen levels decrease, so we are more susceptible."

Barb, now dry-mouthed from talking, dug into her pack and pulled out a raspberry juice. After taking a hearty gulp, she continued, "Smoking also increases one's risk of osteoporosis. I heard on the news last week that teenage girl smokers are on the rise in Canada!"

"I'm sure glad I quit smoking eight years ago," said Liz, "it was an expensive habit that was affecting my lungs, heart and who knows what else. I guess the only good news about being overweight is that I have more bone mass and less likely to get osteoporosis, right?"

"That's true Liz," said Barb, "but being overweight puts you at greater risk for other health problems."

"You're right, Barb," said Liz, in a slightly dejected voice. Then, changing her tone almost immediately, she added, "but I'm trying!"

A west wind blew gently across the tops of the maple trees, causing crimson leaves to fall like raindrops upon the four women seated below. Soon they all started to giggle, then laugh. Within minutes, they tossed leaves at one another. First there were handfuls, then armfuls of leaves flung in every direction. The tall maple trees that surrounded the women looked down to watch them play with their leaves. It was a special time of joy for all! However, it wasn't long before the women were tired out from laughing and playing. Once again they gathered to sit on the piles of fallen leaves.

Sue was a little out of breath, but gasped a comment to her companions anyway, "I'm glad to see... we were all working to prevent... osteoporosis... these past few minutes!" Sue smiled, took another deep breath and pulled a leaf out of her hair.

Kim responded jokingly, "You mean playing leaf tag will help prevent our bones from breaking down?"

The four women smiled in unison. "I mean exercise, Kim," said Sue. "Osteoporosis, for the most part, is preventable. You see," continued Sue, "when we exercise against resistance, we strengthen muscles... and muscles are attached to bones. The muscles pull on the bone, and this makes the bone stronger and more dense."

Kim then asked, "When you say resistance, you mean gravity or weight-bearing exercise?"

"Exactly," answered Sue and continued, "good examples of weight-bearing exercise are walking, lifting weights, or even swimming, when using flippers and hand paddles."

"And don't forget about calcium intakes," reminded Barb, "women should take between 1,000 and 1,500mg daily. The vast majority of daily calcium should come from your diet... and top it off with calcium supplements."

"So what foods are high in calcium, Barb?" asked Liz, who was still brushing pieces of leaves off her coat.

"All your dairy products... like milk, cheese and yogurt... are easy ones to remember," stated Barb. "But leafy green vegetables too, like broccoli and spinach are also rich sources of calcium."

"Salmon is especially high in calcium," added Sue and then said, "because of my mother's osteoporosis, I eat foods high in calcium and work out at the gym three times a week."

Kim's eyes grew large from Sue's comments and asked, "Is osteoporosis hereditary?"

"Oh, no, Kim," answered Sue, "but my mother was at risk because she was a fair-haired woman, with a small bone frame. She didn't like to drink milk, used to smoke a pack of cigarettes a day... and never exercised!" Sue continued to assure her friend, "I also have a small bone frame, but I walk and lift weights to build muscle mass. I eat calcium-rich foods and take a small supplement of calcium each day." Kim nodded her head and smiled, thanking Sue for the information.

"What about taking estrogen supplements to help prevent osteoporosis?" asked Liz, looking at Barb, "I know several teaching colleagues who say they take it to help their bones."

Barb decided to stand up and stretch before answering Liz. "There is still a great deal of controversy about estrogen replacement therapy," noted Barb. "I'm always amazed at how society has turned to medicine to fix every ailment, instead of making healthy lifestyle choices." With that comment, Barb shook her head and continued, "Estrogen is used for some women with advanced osteoporosis. But like Sue said, osteoporosis for the most part, is preventable with a healthy diet and regular exercise!" Barb thought about what she had just finished saying and was silent for several moments before she added, "However, it's a woman's choice whether to take estrogen or not. I guess I feel strongly that she should be informed about the positive and negative effects of taking estrogen. I'm concerned about the women who don't question their doctors."

Kim also stood up and brushed off a few leaves, while saying, "I never really thought about osteoporosis until now. I guess I think of it as a disease that affects older women and old age seems so far away... I just worry about today!"

"In a way you're right, Kim," said Sue cautiously, "but on my way home from work last night, I was thinking about how time seems to go faster as I get older." Sue joined her friends who were standing and said, "Quality old age can be ours, if we take good care of ourselves throughout our lives."

"And don't forget that an angel hovering over your left shoulder also helps," added Liz, as she joined her standing friends.

"Quality old age is something we should all be striving for," said Barb. All four female heads nodded to affirm Barb's comment.

"I'll make a list of high-calcium foods for all of you next week," said Sue. "There is very little I can do to help my own mother with her osteoporosis, but I can help my family and friends from the *silent bone robber* by being proactive and getting the word out!"

"Say, how did we get onto this topic anyway? Oh, ya, now I remember... maple syrup has calcium," Liz said, with a smile.

"Sounds like pancakes for dinner tonight, Liz," teased Barb.

The women's warm laughter among the maple trees signalled it was time to gather their packs, pick up any garbage and start their hike back to the birch grove. The afternoon sun touched their backs as they walked eastward. It was warm and comforting... giving each woman a satisfied feeling. This Wednesday, like the ones before, met each woman's expectations... and more. Their growing friendships, empowering discussions on nature and the nature within each woman were energizing and uplifting, like no force or experience before.

SUE'S LIST OF HIGH CALCIUM FOODS

Milk and Milk Products:

1 cup of skimmed milk . . . . 302 mg
1 cup of whole milk . . . . 291 mg
1 oz mozzarella cheese, part-skim . . . . 207 mg
1 cup ricotta cheese, part-skim . . . . 669 mg
1 cup cottage cheese, 1% low fat . . . . 138 mg
1 cup ice cream, soft serve . . . . 236 mg
1 cup yogurt, low fat with fruit . . . . 345 mg

Fruits and Vegetables:

10 dried figs . . . . 269 mg
1 medium orange . . . . 52 mg
1 cup raisins . . . . 71 mg
1 cup rhubarb, cooked with sugar . . . . 348 mg
1 cup spinach, from frozen . . . . 277 mg
1 spear raw broccoli . . . . 72 mg
1 cup, 144 grams, beet greens . . . . 165 mg
1 cup brussel sprouts, cooked from raw . . . . 56 mg

Breads and Cereals:

1 slice whole wheat bread . . . . 32 mg
1 slice raisin bread . . . . 25 mg
Oatmeal, instant fortified from packet . . . . 163 mg
1 cup Total cereal, with added calcium . . . . 200 mg

Meat and Fish Products:

1 can, 213 grams salmon . . . . 181 mg
1 can, 85 grams sardines . . . . 325 mg
18 large, raw shrimp . . . . 52 mg
1 cup, 213 grams canned crab meat . . . . 137 mg
1 cup, 140 grams poultry . . . . 21 mg

Notes

_____

_____

_____

_____

_____

_____

_____

_____

CHAPTER THREE

Kim finished tucking Kyle into bed with a gentle kiss. Kyle smiled back at his mother, while giving his teddy bear a tight squeeze. "How wonderful and special you are," thought Kim, of her only child. She turned out the light and joined her husband Rob in front of the TV. They sat for some time watching a PBS special on the Galapagos Islands. But finally, Kim gave a long yawn and stretched her arms out, as if to touch the ceiling of their two-storey home. As the credits of the program began, Rob switched off the TV, turned to his wife and asked, "Tired Kim?"

"Ya," she responded, "it's been a long day." It had started early with a meeting of her law colleagues and ended with a new client at 5:00 p.m. There was always more to talk about, but Kim thought that Rob might not be interested in hearing about her work and she was too tired anyway. Kim also knew that she was often bored when Rob spoke at length about his work. She didn't understand engineering and the laws of physics... besides, they had Kyle to talk about together!

"I'm ready for bed, too," said Rob, "I'll go set the coffee for tomorrow morning. Why don't you head off to bed? I'll be up shortly."

Before long, both were settled in bed and cuddling close. Rob's male presence beside Kim grew stronger with each breath. Soon he was caressing her shoulder and arm, then slid his hand to cover her soft breast. She gave a slight sigh as his touch became more demanding and continued its tactile journey down her body. Kim tried to concentrate on Rob's touch, but her mind continued to race about her current court case. Being a woman and a lawyer in the nineties was challenging to say the least. Her thoughts also skipped to thinking about Kyle's new babysitter and her new client at work. Kim wanted to place all these issues on hold and respond to Rob's touch, but her head remained determined to prevent her from focusing on this tactile pleasure. Her body was unresponsive to the gentle kisses on her abdomen.

Finally Rob raised his head and asked, "What's wrong, don't you like this?" The room was dark, but she could clearly see into his eyes. They spoke of want and hurt, all at the same time.

"It's not you, Rob," said Kim, "it's me, I keep thinking about work… maybe I'm just too tired."

There was an uncomfortable pause, which eroded the bond between them. Rob then moved away and said in a sharp voice, "Fine! Let me know when your head can be turned onto me and not your work!" He resettled himself on his right side facing the window.

Kim suddenly felt very guilty, but said nothing further to her husband of nearly seventeen years. She wondered what had changed. Even though their lives had always been busy, they had always tried to make time for themselves. But since Kyle had come along, life had been more hectic and her workload at the office had become more stressful. Kim lay awake thinking about her life.

The Fall wind blew dry leaves against the upstairs windows. It was an eerie sound to listen to and she hoped the weather would not turn sour for tomorrow's hike in the forest. Kim always learned so much from her forest friends. "Tomorrow, yes tomorrow," thought Kim, "it will be better tomorrow!" Although sleep did not come for another hour, when Kim finally did fall asleep, she was dreaming of walking among fallen leaves in a grove of poplar trees.

The next morning, a bright sun shone down on the trees, which stood as honour guards along the Trans-Canada Highway. Kim glanced at her watch and knew she had plenty of time to reach the birch grove by 8:30 a.m. Her early morning had been tense. Rob was quiet, but pleasant and had offered to drop Kyle off at the babysitter on his way to work. She was thankful for the neutral exchange. She did not have time to discuss last night's concern now! They did agree, however, to talk that evening, after Kyle was put to bed. Kim realized how fortunate she was that her husband wanted to take the time to talk and share his feelings with her. Not all of her friends were as blessed to have sensitive male companions! Kim turned the radio on to help distract her thoughts from Rob and to focus on her day of hiking ahead.

Kim arrived several minutes ahead of her walking companions. Falling leaves from the birch trees blew in her direction and landed on her car to welcome their weekly visitor. Kim smiled at this poetic thought and wondered where she would be right now, if her parents had never left Hong Kong. She was a woman who enjoyed change and there was certainly plenty of that in the weather near the Canadian Rockies! As her walking friend Liz would say, "If you don't like the weather at your front door, go to the back door!" She smiled at the image which appeared in her mind.

Just then she glanced to her left and saw Sue's mini-van pulling into the parking lot. Liz was the first to get out, followed by Barb. Liz walked over to Kim's car and as Kim locked the door, Liz said, "Hi, Ms. Lawyer, ready for a full day in the forest?"

Before Kim could respond, Barb called out, "You're early Kim," adjusting her day-pack, while walking over to greet Kim.

Kim decided to answer them both by saying, "I got a good start before traffic and Rob dropped Kyle off at the sitter... Wednesday is the best day of the week, Liz... I wouldn't miss it!"

"Me, too," announced Sue, who was taking up the rear position of the group, "now we can get away in good time." The women gave one another a warm, welcome embrace to energize themselves for the day ahead.

"I think it's your turn to lead Kim," said Barb. "Today we are going to Bengert's Pond... it's on the far north edge of the forest."

"Sounds interesting. Anything special we should be looking out for?" questioned Kim, as she tightened her left boot lace.

Barb answered, "There is a large grassy meadow near the pond. Canada Geese land there and feed, before they go south for the winter. So listen for their distinctive honking sounds." The troop of women smiled in anticipation of discovering new sights and sounds, then set off from the birch grove.

As the women walked along behind Kim, they stopped along the way to admire the coloured vegetation or to take in the crisp smells of Fall air. A slight wind followed the women on their journey up to the north edge of the forest. Every now and then the poplar trees lining their path would shed their yellow leaves in cascades onto the women below. The women smiled at the image of having an outdoor shower of leaves.

Soon the poplar trees gave way to smaller trees and shrubs along the path. Kim, who had continued to lead the group, suddenly stopped and, turning to her friends, exclaimed, "Hear that?" There was no doubt in what they all heard... the honking calls of Canada Geese.

As Liz looked up, she saw the "V" formation slowly descending into a pasture ahead. "I think we're getting close," said an excited Liz.

Nodding her head in agreement, Sue whispered, "Let's be as quiet as we can." She took the camera out of her pack in anticipation of photographing the great birds. Within a few minutes, the women spotted a large, open, grassy field. They decided to stay just inside the shrubs' perimeter, which created a perfect blind from the geese in the pasture.

The women whispered back and forth to each other about what lay before them... several hundred Canada Geese were feeding in the grass. "They're magnificent," exclaimed Liz, "and so big!" Liz's eyes grew large as she expressed her thoughts.

Sue agreed with a nod of her head and then said, "The gander often has a wingspan of one-and-a-half metres and weighs up to six kilograms."

"They're fast flyers, too," interrupted Barb, "they can fly at speeds of up to 72 kilometres per hour."

"Wow," said Kim, as she continued to study the black-necked birds through her binoculars. As Kim found something to share with the others, she said, "Hey, look at that pair... they have some younger geese with them."

"Where?" asked Sue, who was now eagerly searching to find the family of geese.

Kim continued, "Over to the right, near that old tree stump."

"Got it," thanked Sue, "I count eight, lightly feathered, brown goslings!"

"That is so neat!" exclaimed Kim.

Sue was busy photographing with her zoom lens, when Barb said to Kim and Liz, "Canada Geese mate for life and some pairs have lived up to 20 years. They are good parents to their young for almost three-quarters of a year and will protect them with their lives. I imagine those young birds will be with their parents until early Spring, then they will head out on their own." While Barb spoke, Liz and Kim kept their eyes focused on the hundreds of geese before them, but heard every word.

As the women watched for over an hour, they noted that the males and females honked greetings and signals to each other and their young. "I'd say that they have communication all figured out," commented Sue. "They look very contented together as couples, families and a flock!"

"I agree with you, Sue," said Kim, as she lowered the binoculars. "But I wonder if they ever argue or disagree, or what do they do if one of them is having a bad day?" Kim was the kind of woman whose face revealed everything. There were never any hidden agendas with Kim. If she looked puzzled, she was. If she had something on her mind, they all knew it. The question hung in the air, like a kite caught in an updraft.

The three women remained silent, reflecting on Kim's question. Finally, Barb broke the silence. "Are you talking about geese here, or something else?"

"Oh, I don't know, never mind, it's a silly question," answered Kim, "maybe it's time we moved on," putting the question off.

They all agreed and slowly moved back into higher trees. From here, they took a left turn in the trail and walked another ten minutes west of the pasture. Their path ended at a clear, deep blue pond. It was as wide as a house, with trees and shrubs touching the edge of the water. There was a small clearing at the end of the path, where they could walk right down to the water's edge. Looking at the beautiful scene before them, it was difficult to know which was real and which was the perfect reflection. The wind did not follow them to this serene spot. The pond was still and silent, except for the insects which scooted along the top of the water.

Bengert's Pond was named after an older couple who had found the pond on one of their many hikes into the forest. It was a place of peace and serenity… it was Mother Earth herself! "It is also a perfect spot for lunch and conversation," thought Barb, who then raised the question, "Does anyone want to have lunch here?" The response was a chorus of "Yes," "Sure," and "You bet," from the others. Within minutes all were sitting eating their lunches and taking in the beauty.

Barb continued to wonder about Kim's earlier comment and had noticed a stressful expression on her face most of the morning. "Bengert's Pond would be a safe place to talk among friends," thought Barb. And so she began, "Canadian geese are very unique birds," talking to no one in particular. "You raised an interesting question, Kim… do they ever struggle, like many of us do, with communication or intimacy?" The women became more alert and stopped eating to ponder the question placed before them. "Phillip and I had a good marriage," commented Barb, "but there were times when our communication would break down and our intimacy would be affected."

"My husband's workload prevents anything from happening between the sheets in our house," commented Sue. The women, including Sue, all smiled at the thought. Sue then continued, "When life seems to be throwing us curve balls, sometimes we have no time to act. We simply react instead, which is a poor way of dealing with a situation, especially one as complex as relationships."

Liz swallowed her last bite of carrot and asked, "I don't have a husband or partner... isn't arguing just part of a relationship?"

"Rob and I don't argue exactly," commented Kim, "we just have different agendas. Since the birth of Kyle and returning to work at the law office, it seems like I have no time to relax and enjoy intimacy with Rob." Kim continued, "When we are together, I keep thinking about work, or Kyle, or something other than us... it's very frustrating!" Kim looked sad as she spoke those final words.

The women were silent for a few moments. Just then, several dried leaves dropped onto the still pond and created a ripple which moved toward them. The movement of the water was smooth and inviting to watch. Finally, near the edge of the pond, the miniature waves disappeared.

When Kim looked up, Barb was smiling at her with a kind and caring face. "You know, Kim," she started, "having quality intimacy in the nineties has become quite a challenge for many couples."

Sue then broke in, "Sometimes I feel like a rag doll being pulled in all directions at once. We go to work, try to stay healthy and fit, look after our children, manage our homes, volunteer in our church or community and we're still on the go when our husbands come home after work. Finally, we all collapse into bed and the last thing on our mind is making love with our partners!"

Kim was nodding her head in agreement as Sue continued, "My sister, for example, is a very busy woman who would like to spend more time with her husband. But he plays computer games all evening... it's created quite a rift in their relationship."

"Is she going to sue IBM because of what it's doing to their marriage?" joked Liz. "After all, he deserves time to himself, too!"

"That's true," said Sue, "but it just seems that men hardly say two words to us all day, and then suddenly hop into bed and want to make love. Women need to have the mood set ahead of time."

Barb stretched her back before adding, "I think men express themselves physically in most situations, whereas women express themselves more emotionally. Neither way is all right, nor all wrong;

it's just the way most men and women are!"

"Then how in the world are we supposed to get along?" questioned Kim, looking directly at Barb. "Let me give you an example," continued Kim. "Suppose you come home from work with a terrible headache or backache, or just an exhausting day at work... anything which affects the way you feel about yourself."

Sue then added, "When I'm premenstrual, I always feel bloated and fat; I don't feel very feminine."

"Exactly," said Kim, "maybe we could call these issues a... a... dysfunction, just to categorize them for discussion's sake. Anyway," she continued, "I come home from work, start dinner and play with Kyle. I don't feel like doing any of these things, but I do. I remain self-absorbed about this dysfunction, perhaps more quiet than usual and stay in this introverted state all evening. Once in bed, Rob may notice that I'm different tonight... more withdrawn than usual. So Rob may try and make me feel better by having intercourse... his way of showing me that he loves me. My dilemma is that I feel like I'm sinking downward in this spiral and I have no control to stop it. As I lie in bed, I recall how I dropped a glass while cleaning up after dinner and hurried Kyle through his bath. I also snapped at Rob several times during the evening. I want to be perfect, you know," said Kim with a pleading look to her friends.

"We *all* do," said Sue, "that's what creates our problems! We want to be superwomen and do it all."

Each woman quietly took stock of how many times she wanted to say NO, to her children, spouse or friends, but did not. Kim continued, "My self-concept is low and I plunge even farther, using negative talk in a damaging way. I do not feel feminine or attractive. I might say to myself, 'I'm such a loser... I should have handled that court case more professionally.' I'm right in the middle of this destructive self-talk and suddenly I feel his touch! At this point, I sometimes say to myself, 'Why does he want to love me. Can't he see that I'm a poor lawyer, mother and wife?' I hurt and I hate myself... and him for wanting to love me. I lie unresponsive to his touch, full of self-pity and anger. Finally, I touch bottom and I either turn over in bed away from him or make a remark that rejects him and his love. The intimacy that could have happened has been destroyed. Rob is frustrated and angry with me and I remain over-burdened in my head with tasks undone and feel very, very guilty!"

Liz took a small stick that was near her and started drawing in the mud near the pond. As she drew the image of a spiral, she spoke. "It sounds like we have just travelled down a spiral, starting with a dysfunction, leading to self-absorption, lack of communication and lowered self-concept, then to self-destructive behaviours, ending with the destruction of intimacy."

Each woman looked at the spiral that Liz had drawn in the mud. Sue then spoke, "It would seem that most days we simply sail along on a straight line... some ups and some downs... but I can certainly relate to many of those nose-dive spirals you have just spoken about, Kim."

Barb had been deep in thought. She then took a deep breath and said, "Before Phillip died, he was often really down."

"Were you able to help him?" asked Kim.

"Well," started Barb, "early in his cancer experience, he started to have pain and he didn't want to say anything to upset me. He would come home from the office and be quiet and withdrawn. I could tell something was wrong, but decided to let him have his space and let him deal with this in his own way. But that made it worse! We would go to bed and I would roll over and kiss him... he would say very little... finally, he would reject me, saying that he was too tired to make love. This was a very painful time in my life. We both knew that we had only a few months left together and being intimate would comfort us both."

"Oh, Barb," said Kim, "that must have been so hard on you." Kim now moved over to touch her friend's arm and give her an encouraging smile. Sue and Liz also gathered close. It was as though this serene place understood the sensitive topic the women discussed and, like a mother, wrapped her beauty around them... giving them love and support.

Feeling strengthened by her friends, Barb continued, "I told our minister about the situation and she helped a great deal. After some counselling sessions, I decided to change tactics. From then on, when Phillip would appear down, we would sit and talk or go for a quiet walk. We worked harder on our communication. I told him I needed to know what was happening with him so I could help... not as a nurse, but as his best friend. Later when we went to bed... because there were no hidden agendas... we would touch, kiss and just hold each other. I would tell him as many positive things about him as I could... to help build his self-confidence and prevent him from going down. You see, he was afraid of disappointing me during our intimacy. He needed to know when he was feeling unwell or in pain, or the dysfunction as Kim calls it, that cuddling close, touching and kissing is OK... we do not have to have intercourse to be intimate. That relieved him a great deal."

Barb looked directly at the pond and spoke further, "You see, whatever you do as a couple to affirm your love for each other is good for you both."

Liz looked down at the spiral she had drawn in the mud. "So," she began, "if you intercede with communication, which helps affirm the partner as a whole, sexual being, you could prevent him or her from dipping down into lowered self-concept, self-destructive behaviours and the destruction of intimacy. It sounds like you broke down the spiral by using communication, Barb," said Liz, as she smiled at her tawny-skinned friend.

"Well, it worked for us," smiled Barb, "I hope it can work for others." Barb looked directly at Kim and said, "What do you think, Kim?"

"I'd like to give it a try all right," replied Kim, "but I'm the one who often has the dysfunction, so I need to have Rob understand how I feel when I start this downward spiral." Kim thought of the many times she would not tell Rob about her day, nor share some of her thoughts and feelings with him. She also thought of the many times, when he would be telling her about his day, that her thoughts would drift somewhere else. Kim looked into the pond and saw her reflection staring back at her. Just then, two large Canada Geese flew above the pond. Their wing span appeared even larger in the water's reflection. The women did not look skyward, but followed the grace of the lifelong, mated pair across the pond. As the giant birds passed by, the women found themselves staring at their own image in Bengert's Pond. Each knew her own abilities, disabilities or dysfunctions.

Kim's oriental features were sharp and clear in the water, like her new-found focus on how she could improve the intimacy between herself and Rob. She needed to learn to tell him how she felt, share her fears and concerns. Then, when it was time to be close with one another... each could give the other what was needed. Moments passed into minutes before each woman awoke from her private thoughts. It would be difficult to leave the pond today because it had become a safe place to share thoughts of intimacy. In fact, it was intimacy!

The sun started to play hide-and-seek between the high clouds and the women knew it was time to leave. Canada Geese continued to fly overhead; a few followed the path that the women took back to the birch grove. It had been a very growthful day. The walk back seemed to take only minutes, as each woman remained deep in thought. Kim waved goodbye to her friends as she pulled out of the parking lot. Fallen leaves stirred up behind the car as she drove away. Rob and Kyle were waiting for her at the door when she drove up to her home. They both had loving smiles and warm hugs to welcome her. After Kyle was put to bed, Kim and Rob talked well into the evening about sharing their feelings. Before sleep came to either of them, they were passionate in their intimacy, affirming what they felt for each other. Kim slept a peaceful sleep that night and dreamed of a serene, still pond... a safe place of intimacy.

LIZ'S SUMMARY

DESTRUCTIVE BEHAVIOURS IN SEXUAL INTIMACY

Dysfunction

Self-Absorption

Lack of Communication

Lowered Self-Concept

Self Destructive Behaviours

Destruction of Intimacy

MODEL OF DESTRUCTIVE BEHAVIOURS IN INTIMACY

1. **Dysfunction:** This could be a disappointment, acute or chronic pain, stress, premenstrual tension, a bad day at work, a headache. Anything which affects the way you feel about yourself or others.

2. **Self-Absorption:** Introverted and/or obsessive thoughts about the dysfunction. One does not focus clearly on other issues concerning self or others.

3. **Lack of Communication:** Due to self-absorption, individual talks very little about dysfunction to partner. Individual is quiet and withdrawn.

   * The partner could intercede at this time to prevent further deterioration. Person with dysfunction needs support, encouragement and to be validated as a worthy person.

4. **Lowered Self-Concept:** Individual no longer feels feminine or masculine. She/he may be filled with a sense of shame or hopelessness. The individual feels unworthy of receiving love and affection from partner.

5. **Self-Destructive Behaviour:** The individual uses negative self-talk, which is very damaging. Example: "I am a terrible wife," or " I hate the way I look." Individual may try to harm self.

6. **Destruction of Intimacy:** Individual now directs the destructive talk towards partner. Refuses or rejects companionship… then feels guilty. Verbal abuse may take place.

Model of Destructive Behaviour in Sexual Intimacy
Copyright 1993
Linda J. Ormson R.N.

CHAPTER FOUR

It was past 4:30 p.m. on Tuesday afternoon, when Liz finished marking the last of her grade five spelling tests. As Liz recorded ten-year-old Brad's below-average mark, she wondered how this young student and she would manage the remaining eight months of the year. Liz had already had one parent-teacher interview with Brad's mother. She claimed that "Brad does whatever he wants... I've never been able to control him!" Liz thought about last week's incident when Brad set fire to another student's school books. It would seem, thought Liz, that Brad had not learned one of the basic lessons about living within a community... to respect other people, their feelings and their possessions.

Liz had rescued the crying student whose books had been sacrificed so early in the school year. When turning to give Brad a stern scolding, Liz was met with a shower of profane language which was sharp and corrosive. And perhaps worse, at least to Liz, this incident had set off a series of hot flashes which seemed to be never ending. Sometimes when Liz felt stressed, she would experience a sensation of heat rising from the upper half of her body. It lasted only 10 – 20 seconds, but to Liz, it seemed an intolerable amount of time. Immediately afterward, she would perspire and experience chills from the leftover damp feeling. This event had recently come about with the beginning of the school year and seemed to coincide with

Brad's overt behaviour.

Liz shook her head from side to side, as if to shake away the negative images and began to tidy up her desk. She wrote out the instructions for her substitute teacher, Anne, who took the class for her each Wednesday. Thanks to a flexible principal and an excellent substitute teacher, Liz could take the extra day each week to nurture herself. As she finished her note to Anne, she saw the familiar janitor's broom being pushed down the hall… it was getting late and time to go.

Driving home, she took in some deep breaths and slowly let the air escape through her pursed lips. It was her way of trying to let go of troublesome little boys and regain some energy for tomorrow's walk in the forest. Liz's body had always reacted negatively to perceived stressors and, though therapy had helped her a great deal throughout the years, she still struggled with the physical reaction to stressful situations. Perhaps menopause was going to be a challenge too!

As Liz pulled into the driveway, she could see the lights on in her mother's room. Her 82-year-old mother was mentally sharp, but her debilitating arthritis prevented her from moving about. Liz had the Victorian Order of Nurses come in during the day to provide some basic care and meals for her mother. Liz provided for the remainder of her mother's needs. The two women had lived together their entire life. First as mother and daughter, then after Liz's father died, a closer bond developed between them and they became good friends.

After tucking her car into the garage for the night, she started making dinner for the two of them. Before long, a pasta dish with side salad and French bread was served. Liz and her mother, Florence, enjoyed their meal and light conversation. However, when Liz served some steamy, hot coffee to have with their leftover apple strudel, she once again experienced the feeling of heat rising up and overwhelming her. "Oh, how I hate this," exclaimed Liz, as she threw her napkin onto the table.

Florence was surprised at her daughter's outburst and asked, "What's wrong, Elizabeth?" using her daughter's given name.

Liz looked directly at her mother and answered, "It's these hot flashes... did my face go all red, Mom?"

"Why no, you look just fine," said Florence, who reached out for her daughter's hand. Despite the appearance of the disjointed and inflamed fingers, her touch was soothing to Liz. Florence smiled warmly at her only child and said, "I know what you are going through. I remember getting hot flashes when I was your age. I would dash off to the nearest bathroom to check out my face in the mirror... and to my surprise, little rosy cheeks, that's all!"

Liz sat straighter in her kitchen chair, took a deep breath and said, "You mean, I'm the only one who knows?"

Florence had a great deal of love and respect for her daughter and wanted to answer as truthfully as she could, "I think so dear. Worrying about menopause only makes it worse... it's a natural part of growing older... it's part of life. Would you like to talk about it, dear... sometimes that can help?" Liz smiled at her mother in appreciation for her support, but thought that her mother really didn't know what she was going through and Liz didn't want to talk or think about growing old... at least not now.

Before long, the kitchen was tidied up and both women prepared for bed. Liz slept well until about 3:00 a.m., when she woke up soaking wet. It was like someone had played a nasty trick and dumped a bucket of warm water over her. "Night sweats," thought Liz, as she got out of bed, "more night sweats!" She sponged herself down, put on a dry nightgown and changed her sheets, so that by 3:30 a.m., she was back into a fresh bed.

Liz awoke to music from the radio alarm at 6:45. It had been a restless sleep, dreaming of her mother and a naughty little boy! But her shower was hot and cleansing and soon removed any thought of last night's damp experience. As Liz lathered her body, she thought of the hike she would take with her forest friends. These women had become close companions who shared their thoughts and feelings with each other. She always felt so refreshed after her Wednesdays. Liz yawned as she quickly dressed, thinking that she needed today, more than ever, to refresh her spirit. After packing her lunch and saying goodbye to her mother, Liz drove out from the driveway.

The drive west was relaxing as Liz listened to a radio station which played music from the 70s and 80s. The triad of radio hosts was entertaining between the music and Liz smiled at their wholesome fun. By 8:30 a.m., Liz pulled into the parking lot at the birch grove. Sue, Barb and Kim had also just arrived. Within minutes, the four women had gathered their day packs and were preparing to hike into the forest. Sue gave a long stretch, raising her arms upward. "Oh, that feels so good," she exclaimed. Her eyes followed to the tips of her fingers and beyond to the nearby tree tops. "Wow," she exclaimed, "have those trees ever turned colour since last week! They must have had more frost out here… I can see all the branches!"

Barb took a long look at the tree tops before saying to her friends, "I think we'll only have a few more weeks of hiking before we get snow."

The other three women all turned to Barb, but Kim spoke first. "Let's not rush the season… please Barb, I look forward to our Wednesdays so much."

"OK, Kim," said Barb, wanting to relieve the frown that had formed on Kim's face, "but winter is coming!" Barb's comment hung in the air like the bare branches on the trees before them. They all knew that Barb was right, but wanted to postpone it as long as possible.

To break the solemn moment, Sue asked, "Where are we going to hike today, Barb?"

Barb turned to answer, "There is a large grove of oak trees on the southeast perimeter of the forest. We have to go up a few fairly steep hills… most oaks like high ground."

"I'm ready for a challenge," said Kim in a frisky voice.

"Me, too," said Sue.

"How about you, Liz?" asked Barb.

"I'm feeling a little like Fall today," said Liz, "but count me in." With that comment, the other three women surrounded Liz and gave her an energizing group hug. The smiles, back rubs and squeezing arms were all gratefully received and welcomed by Liz.

The women of the forest followed one behind the other along the winding path. Barb led the way, using her topographical map and following the trail signs. It was still early and a cloud-like mist hung near the ground, shrouding the lower bushes. They headed south through the birch trees with their paper-like, white bark. The contrast of the yellowing foliage and the peeling layers of thin, white bark was a perfect example of just how unique this forest was. The women were silent as they walked along, each breathing in the spectacle that lay before them. After walking for only fifteen minutes, Barb suddenly stopped, creating a domino effect on her walking companions... each bumping into one another. "Shh," motioned Barb, placing her finger to her lips. She pointed ahead. The women's eyes searched beyond Barb's extended arm. As the women focused on the large, dark brown object to the right of the path, they all gasped. "A moose," whispered Kim... "wow." They all stood motionless, watching the 350-kilogram female browse on the birch twigs. This largest member of the deer family had a long face, overlapping upper lip, large ears and a large dewlap of skin hanging from her throat. The hump on her back was quite pronounced as she nibbled lower to tear off some of the remaining green vegetation. The women continued to watch in silence. However, Barb was scouting out another path to take them around this large mammal, which was consuming her morning breakfast. Without saying a word, Barb motioned to Kim, who was standing right behind her, to follow. Barb lead the women to the far left of the well-worn path. It was difficult to walk among the dense bushes. A few minutes into the detour, Liz tripped over a fallen branch; but fortunately, she regained her balance before landing head first in a caragana bush. It took almost twenty minutes before they returned to the path. They were now far ahead of the still browsing moose, who seemed undisturbed by their presence. As the women emerged onto the trail, Barb asked, "Everyone OK? How about you, Liz?"

"Oh, I scraped my leg back there... but I'm fine." Liz smiled back at Barb to reassure her.

Sue and Kim were brushing off a few burrs that had attached themselves to their clothing. Kim spoke as she picked off the last sticky hitchhiker. "That's one… big… animal, but she didn't seem to mind us… maybe we could have just walked right by her, instead of taking the detour."

"I don't think so," answered Barb, "I'm sure she knew we were there… and besides, this is rutting season. If Mr. Moose happened to be around, he'd see us as prime competition."

Kim's eyes grew large, thinking about the possibility. "Maybe we should put a little more distance between us and Ms. Moose," said Kim, "just in case." All four heads nodded and they continued their hike, following Barb south along the path.

The women hiked for another two hours. As Barb had said earlier, they would climb a few hills. After they left the female moose among the birch trees, the women encountered their first oak trees. These had broad trunks with a large crown of branches and leaves. The hiking trail widened as they reached the top of one of the highest hills in the forest. Kim and Sue spotted a large boulder near the summit and without saying a word, they dashed off to see who would get there first. "Is that the finish line?" asked an exhausted Liz, as she watch the two energetic women running to capture the large piece of granite.

Barb extended her hand out to Liz and said, "Yup… and you made it too, Liz!" Liz and Barb walked the final steps together to reach Kim and Sue, who were now sitting on the huge rock laughing.

"So who won *Capture the Rock*?" questioned a tired Liz.

"We both did," answered an out-of-breath Kim. All of the women smiled, knowing the joy of being able to play and have fun.

It was now shortly after noon. Within minutes, they were all unpacking their lunches and finding comfortable spots to sit and eat their meal. There was a steady west wind on the hilltop, which was refreshing after their earlier walk in the damp birch grove. And, to make it more pleasant, it was also bright and sunny. It had been a long and fairly arduous hike and the women were hungry. They had finished their lunch before they began to survey their surroundings.

Sue swallowed her last bite of a whole-wheat bagel and then asked, "Do all oaks live on hilltops?"

"Mostly, yes," answered Barb. "They try to capture lots of sunlight and like well-drained soil... although, there are a few species of oak that like swampy, wet terrains." She continued, "I believe there are ten species of oaks that grow in Canada... except for this special forest, most grow in the east." Barb took a long swallow of Diet Coke and then added, "The fruit of the oak is the acorn, which is important for the diets of a variety of wild animals."

Liz commented, "Actually the acorn is edible and was often cooked and eaten by native Canadians to supplement their diet. The oil, which can be extracted, was used to rub on and soothe painful joints."

"That's really interesting," said Kim, as she leaned over and picked up a fallen acorn. It was smaller than a twenty-five-cent piece and about one quarter of it was enclosed in a bowl-shaped cup, covered with knob-like brownish scales. After Kim had looked at the nut, she passed it over to Liz, who was sitting next to her. Liz rolled the nut around the palm of her hand, guided by her fingers. Over half of the nut was smooth to the touch and the other portion was very rough. The other women watched Liz fondle the little package from nature.

When Liz noticed that her friends were watching her, she said, "You know this nut kind of reminds me of my skin... once it was all smooth like this end and the other end feels like my skin right now!" They all smiled at the analogy and then Liz continued, "Actually, that moose we saw earlier today could be called 'Elizabeth,' I'm sure that's how I'm going to look in a few years!" Liz became animated using her hands to help explain her further comments. "You know... the hump at the back, extra skin hanging from my neck." Liz even made a long face to imitate her four-legged sister.

"Oh, come on Liz," said Barb... "growing old is not that bad."

Liz looked directly at Barb and said, "Well, getting there is no piece of cake!"

"So what's up?" asked the perceptive Kim, "Are you afraid of wrinkles and grey hair?"

Liz tucked the remainder of her lunch into her backpack, then looked back at Kim and answered. "It's these hot flashes… they're driving me crazy!" Liz sat with an exasperated expression on her face.

"Hot flashes?" asked Kim.

Barb gently touched Kim's arm to get her attention and then explained. "Women describe hot flashes as a sensation of heat rising from the upper chest into the face."

"You can say that again," interrupted Liz.

Barb sent a warm smile toward Liz before continuing, "Some women experience hot flashes while going through menopause, but many do not. In fact, some hot flashes are so mild, women assume that it's just a hot room, too many blankets or a change in the weather. I never paid much attention to mine, perhaps that is why they never really bothered me."

"What causes hot flashes?" asked Kim, directing her question at Barb.

"Well no-one is exactly sure," answered Barb, "but because estrogen production in a woman's mid-to-late forties declines, the pituitary gland may send out signals to the body for it to produce more estrogen. During a hot flash, blood vessels dilate and constrict irregularly and unpredictably. It is believed that the hot flash may be the body's attempt to answer the pituitary gland."

Liz listened to every word her nurse friend spoke and then said in a joking tone of voice, "Well, my body certainly likes to respond… I had two hot flashes yesterday!"

"My sister claims that hot spicy food sets hers off," interjected Sue, "Is that possible?"

Barb nodded her head and answered, "Many times they are triggered by spicy foods, hot drinks or even alcohol and… stressful situations."

Liz took a deep breath and blew it out forcefully and then said to her friends, "I've been really trying to slow down this Fall. My Wednesdays off have been helpful, but my class has several challenging students this term and I worry about my mother." Liz's eyes began to fill with tears.

The women could relate to the busy schedules of living in the nineties and the strain of families and relationships. Sue placed her arm around Liz's shoulder to provide support to her walking companion. She had been gathering a few acorns into a pile in front of her. Sue was the most physically fit of the four and worked hard at being in touch with her body. At age 45, recently she had noticed some of the subtle changes that occur when women's estrogen levels begin to decrease. Her menstrual periods were now heavier and longer in duration... and were about 21 days apart. Sue also noticed that she sometimes needed vaginal lubricant before she had intercourse with her husband.

After giving an additional squeeze to Liz's shoulder, Sue commented, "I've been reading a fair bit lately about menopause, mostly so I will understand what changes I can expect." The three other women now turned their attention to Sue. "I've read that there are only three signs directly related to the changes in the estrogen production." Sue raised her left hand and used her fingers to count off as she spoke, "One... changes in the menstrual cycle... two, hot flashes and sweats... three, vaginal dryness." After returning her hand to her lap, she further said, "There seem to be more myths than facts out there about menopause."

"Like what?" asked Kim, who then changed into a squatting position, almost on top of Sue's pile of acorns.

"Like the raging hormone myth," continued Sue, "which describes menopausal women as incapable of rational thought, depressed, having poor memory, mood swings and relationship problems. When I think of what is going on in women's lives during their 40s and early 50s, it's not surprising that some of these things are a reality of living today... not necessarily because of menopause!" Sue wanted to make one final point to the women of the forest before she placed the final acorn on top of the pile. "I really believe that if women could move past our cultural stereotype of menopausal women, we might not spend so much time blaming everything on menopause!"

Kim guided Sue's hand to help place the nut on the miniature mountain. "It's interesting that you spoke of culture, Sue," said Kim, "because in the Chinese culture, older women are valued for their wisdom and the stability that they bring to the extended family. In fact, the older one is, the more one is revered... kind of like that old oak tree over there." Kim turned to Barb and asked, "What do you think, Barb?"

Barb thought for several moments and then answered, "When our mothers went through menopause, there was very little information on the topic available. Perhaps they only knew what other women told them... which could be positive or negative. Today, many women **buy in** so to speak, to the popular cultural beliefs that menopause is a negative experience. I would agree with you, Sue. They may not be dealing with the real reason for their behaviours."

"Now, hold on you two," said Liz in a demanding voice, "are you saying that if I perceive menopause to be a positive experience, it will be?" Liz began to shake her head from side to side before she continued, "My hot flashes are real and darned unpleasant!"

"All we're saying, Liz," said Sue, "is that it is important to understand how each woman perceives change... because that does affect how each one deals with it... positively or negatively. You're the one who brought up the subject of Ms. Moose, remember!"

"OK, OK," said Liz, with a slight grin on her face, "so I need an attitude adjustment... help me!" With that comment, a pleading look went out to her friends.

Barb turned her attention to a large oak tree across the little meadow from where they sat. Its sturdy trunk held a huge crown of golden leaves. "See that oak over there," said Barb to Liz, as she pointed to the tree that Kim had mentioned earlier. Liz and the other women followed Barb's finger. "Oaks are known for their strength and longevity, as Kim mentioned. Their wood is very hard, so it's in high demand for building. The Druids of England revered the oak as a symbol of fertility, stability and strength. It was also a symbol of the earth's renewal... because it stood for the changes of the seasons.

Like oaks," Barb continued, "women are strong and live long lives. They are the givers of life and have many changes to go through... from puberty to menopause." Barb was silent for a minute, while she stared at the oak tree and then made a final comment, "Menopause is an important physical and emotional change. We are all different after we go through it... perhaps even better!"

Liz had fixed her eyes on the tree that had come to represent *women* on this day of discovery. She chose her words carefully and spoke slowly, "Perhaps you're right, Barb. Women can be strengthened and empowered by appreciating the realities of their own experiences and by supporting other women during this time in their lives. My mother was trying to tell me that last night during dinner, but I wasn't listening or wanting to believe her... perhaps I don't value my mother's opinions, because she is old!"

"Don't be too hard on yourself, Liz," said Kim. "Cultural stereotypes are hard to break, but we could start by sharing and listening to other women... all women, regardless of age."

As the women continued to watch the golden oak leaves being tossed about by the wind, they thought about Kim's final comment. A gust of cool air blew in their direction, sending leaves scattering among the women. The large slab of granite was warm from the sun, so they climbed up to regain their lost heat. From high above, a soaring hawk looked down to see four women sitting cross-legged in a circle. Somehow it seemed like a natural sight to the bird of prey... women, one with the earth!

Kim had taken a large, red apple out of her bag and cut it into four pieces to share with her friends. Handing a quarter of the apple to Barb, she asked, "So should women take estrogen replacement therapy during menopause?"

"Well," Barb replied, "first I think it's important to know that when a woman's ovaries no longer produce enough hormones to trigger the release of eggs, or to build up menstrual blood, both ovulation and menstruation stop. But there are other sources of estrogen. It is stored in the fatty tissues of our body and small amounts continue to be excreted from our ovaries for at least another ten years after menopause."

Liz brightened up with that comment and said, "You mean I've got estrogen right here?" pinching her stomach to make a generous bulge. Laughter erupted and poured into the valley below.

When the last giggles subsided, Barb continued, "Our adrenal glands are also a source of estrogen." The look on Kim's face was one giant question mark, so Barb answered before Kim could ask. "The adrenal glands sit on top of our kidneys. Their job is to help us cope with stress and maintain our resistance to disease. As estrogen slowly declines, our adrenal glands gradually take over to become our major source of estrogen after menopause. It's rather complicated, but there is a conversion from one type of hormone into estrogen."

"I've read that, too," exclaimed Sue, "and exercise helps speed up the conversion process."

"Eating foods high in Vitamins B and C as well as limiting your coffee, alcohol and sweets, also helps reduce stresses on the adrenals." said Barb, "You see, the ovarian source of estrogen provides additional protection for a woman's heart, digestive system, lungs, bones and skin... now it has to come from the adrenal source." Barb began eating the piece of apple that Kim had offered her several minutes before.

Kim had long finished eating hers, so asked, "But is the adrenal source of estrogen enough?"

Barb swallowed a piece of Macintosh apple and thought for several moments before answering. "That's a tough question, Kim, because each woman is unique with respect to her lifestyle choices and the amount of estrogen she produces."

"When you say lifestyle choices, Barb," asked Kim, "do you mean regular exercise, a good diet and not smoking?"

"Exactly," said Barb, "women who smoke usually enter menopause several years before nonsmokers."

Kim still looked puzzled about the "should women take estrogen" question, so Barb continued, "Hormone replacement therapy can be used to treat hot flashes, night sweats and vaginal dryness. However, many women find these symptoms a minor bother. For the vast majority of women, these annoying symptoms stop within one year of their final period anyway. But when symptoms seriously interfere with one's daily life and if non-medical alternatives do not help... a gynaecologist is who you should see."

Sue interrupted, "Apparently if a woman has heart disease or advanced osteoporosis, hormone replacement therapy may add some quality years to her life. But like everything, there are risks too!"

"That's right, Sue," said Barb, "research so far reveals that when women take hormone replacement therapy, their chances of breast and ovarian cancer do increase... but long-term research is still being done and we may not know the results for another ten years."

"I'm not sure I can wait that long," said Liz, "what do I do in the meantime?"

"Take control where you can," said Sue, grabbing both of Liz's hands in hers. "Reduce your stress, relax, drink herbal tea, exercise... forget coffee and dreadful little boys!" The women all laughed at Sue's comment. "Knowledge is power, Liz, so learn what is happening to you and share it with other women... we can all help each other." Liz was thankful for Sue's advice and smiled back at the fit, forty-five year old. After a final squeeze of their hands, Liz did consciously let go of some of her stress!

The sun was still warm and comforting as the women continued their discussion on menopause. "My doctor told me that most women experience perimenopause... the first symptoms of decreased estrogen... starting in their early forties," said Liz, "and on average, menopause starts around age 51... I'm right on!"

"Well, I'm all done," said Barb, "and I feel so free!" The other women thought that Barb had a very peaceful look on her face when she said those words.

"And I'm getting there too," said Sue, who then looked over at Kim. "And you'll be tagging along in about 10 years, Kim." Sue gave an affectionate smile at Kim.

"Yes," said Kim, "but all of you will have shared some of your own personal experiences with me, so I'm going to be well informed when I go through menopause!" The smiling faces of the women were an affirming promise, as they sat holding hands in a circle on the large, hardened piece of earth.

It was a wonderful thought to end their day... thinking of being together for years ahead... and spending afternoons like this one, sharing their own stories with each other. It was nearly 2:30 p.m. when they started their hike down from the oak grove. Before long, they were back in the white-barked birch trees and nearing the parking lot. There was no sign of the female moose they had encountered earlier that morning... Kim was especially glad. And so was Liz, for she no longer pictured the moose as an image of growing older. Instead, she envisioned the sturdy long-lived oak, which symbolized the power and beauty of women... willing to meet the challenges of change and see the passing of the seasons with strength and dignity.

Notes

CHAPTER FIVE

There was very little traffic on the highway west of the city. Sue glanced at her watch. It was shortly after 8:00 a.m. and she had plenty of time before reaching the birch grove. The rolling foothills had a heavy frost during the night and the sun's reflection off the glistening, white blanket was blinding. With her right hand, Sue retrieved her sunglasses from the dashboard of her mini-van. The brilliant light was now subdued. The sunglasses made driving easier, but also darkened her spirits.

Her thoughts wandered back to several days ago, when she had come home from work around 5:00 p.m. Sue encountered a mountain of shoes in her front doorway. She recognized those of her youngest daughter... Dawn. Coats were also scattered about the living room and loud music was blaring from her daughter's bedroom. When Sue entered the kitchen, it was a war zone of open cupboards, microwave pizza boxes and dirty dishes, piled high.

Before leaving work, her one thought was to come home, sit with her feet up and enjoy a hot cup of herbal tea. This mess had spoiled all that. She could feel her anger beginning to grow inside. Sue had always put her family's needs before hers. She enjoyed taking care of her family, but lately it seemed that they did not appreciate all she did for them. Only recently had she taken the job at the coffee shop to get her out of the house and to subsidize the cost of her fitness classes.

Sue's own mother had warned her, "You're spoiling them, Sue. Why don't you let them make their own lunches?"

Sue's response to that comment was, "But they're so unorganized. They would never get to school or work on time without my help... besides, that's part of my job as a mother and a wife... isn't it?"

And then there was last Saturday... a day when all the family normally pitches in to clean the house. Everyone except Sue seemed to have plans which could not be postponed, leaving Sue to clean the house by herself. She wanted to tell them "NO," your chores come first, but she found herself saying "YES." Her husband Brian had escaped to the office, claiming that he had to finish several memos before Monday. Sue had consoled herself by saying that no-one could clean the house as well as she could anyway. And, besides, Brian had promised to take her out for a late lunch.... her reward for being the martyr.

But Brian did not return home until late afternoon. Furthermore, when he finally arrived home after 4:00 p.m., he smelled of alcohol. "I met some friends in the parking lot at the office," he said. "We went for a couple of beers. I didn't think you would mind!" Sue remembered feeling angry and hurt at the same time. Perhaps if she had tighter control over her family, they would not disappoint her so much.

The roar of the mini-van's engine interrupted Sue's thoughts. Her heart was racing, as was the van. She quickly refocused on the speedometer and read... 120 kilometres... "Too fast... too fast," she thought. She immediately took her foot off the accelerator and the van soon returned to the cruising speed of 100 kilometres per hour. Beads of perspiration had formed on Sue's forehead. She took several deep breaths to calm herself. "What am I doing?" she thought, "I must be crazy. Wednesday's are the highlight of my week. Why am I thinking about all these frustrations with my family?"

Sue took one final deep breath and tensed her body, as if to deny any further escape of these negative thoughts from her being. "I am not going to have them ruin my day with my friends!" announced

Sue in a loud voice to the interior of her van. She then reached for one of her favourite tapes and placed it into the cassette recorder. Johann Pachelbel, Kanon D, soon enveloped her vehicle. She had turned the volume up so that its calming affect would penetrate both her body and her mind.

By the time Sue pulled into the parking lot at the birch grove, she had calmed herself considerably. She turned off the motor of her van and just sat there, continuing her newly-relaxed state. Many of the birch trees were now bare of leaves. But the sun shone brightly on the frost-bitten leaves, which were piled on the ground. The early morning sunbeams also lightened Sue's mood, despite her concerns about her family. She remembered that earlier in the day, her children had given her warm hugs and wished her a great day with her friends in the forest. Brian had said he would be waiting for her when she got home. Sue smiled... it was going to be a good day!

Sue turned her head slightly to the left to notice two cars pulling up side by side. Kim and Liz had come out together and Barb had driven alone. Before leaving her car, Sue thought about Barb as a single person. "I'm sure she must get lonely some days. But every now and then, there are moments when I wish I could be alone." But that thought made her fearful and Sue instantly experienced a sudden shiver, shaking her back into reality.

The four women greeted each other with healthy, long-lasting hugs. "How was your drive out, Sue?" asked Barb and then continued. "Sorry I couldn't pick you up, but I stayed at my sister's last night.... she lives in the north end of the city."

Sue placed her arm around Barb's shoulder, remembering her thoughts of Barb a few minutes ago. "It was fine, Barb, I put on one of my favourite pieces of music... do you know Johann Pachelbel, Kanon D?" Barb's eyes sparkled when the seventeenth century composer's name was mentioned.

"I sure do and that particular piece of music has been studied a great deal. Many believe that when it plays, the listener releases endorphins,... morphine-like receptors in the brain. They help boost your immune system, reduce any physical pain, make you feel good and calm you down."

"Well that's exactly why I played it," said Sue, "to calm my nerves and to get focused for today's hike." A warm, contented smile sped across Sue's face.

Barb wanted to ask Sue what she was stressed about, but was interrupted by Kim, who asked, "So where are we off to today, Barb?" Kim was pulling a heavy sweater over her head and the last part of her question was muffled. As her head poked out, she giggled at herself, "Sorry Barb, but *I'm* cold."

Barb smiled at her friend and said, "I thought we could hike over to the west side of the forest today. The tip of this forest touches the first range of the Rocky Mountains... they're called the Continental Ranges." She then pointed to the creek nearby and said, "This creek starts from that mountain range as a few tiny drops of melted snow, which then thread their way down the mountain until they unite. Our creek runs alongside the trail and we can follow it all the way up to the falls."

"Falls... like in water falls?" exclaimed Liz, as she stepped closer to Barb. "I love water falls!" Liz held an excited expression on her face for several seconds. Then it suddenly disappeared as she asked, "I suppose that means we have to climb some steep hills again, like last week?"

"Ya," said Barb nodding her head, "but you did great last week, Liz and besides water falls have to *fall* from somewhere."

"Naturally," said Liz in a slightly sarcastic tone of voice.

"Actually, Liz," said Barb, "you'll hardly notice the slow climb and believe me when you get there, you won't be sorry!"

"OK, Barb, you've convinced me," said Liz, whose smile had returned to her face.

"Can we have lunch at the falls?" asked an enthusiastic Kim.

Barb delighted in her friend's excitement. "Let's make it a date... lunch at the falls," announced Barb and adjusted her day pack for the walk which lay ahead.

The women were all wearing extra clothing, due to the cool morning air, but the sun warmed their backs as they followed Barb away from the birch grove. To their left, the bubbling sound of fresh, cold water accompanied them… except the water was travelling in the opposite direction. They were on this side of the Great Divide and all the water was heading east. The water hurried past them, trying to get to some unknown destination. They heard very few sounds on this cool Fall morning. Many of the fallen leaves on the trail were damp from the frost, so the women's footsteps made no sounds, unlike a few weeks before. There was just the peace of Mother Earth!

The trail wandered through 25-metre-tall white spruce trees. They all stopped to admire these grand specimens. "I'd have to own a big home to set these trees up for Christmas," said Liz jokingly, as she walked over and plucked a few green needles from a low branch. As Liz rubbed the needles between her fingers, they gave off a familiar scent. "Smells like Christmas," said Liz, holding the crushed needles in the palm of her hand.

Sue came over to sniff the needles Liz was holding and said, "Just imagine how beautiful this area will be in another month, when its all covered with snow." Just then a slight gust of wind blew past the four women, making then all shiver with the thought of winter approaching.

Kim was the first to notice a small dirt path, which led off from the main trail, down toward the creek. "I'm going down here for a few minutes," called Kim, to the other women. They smiled at Kim's adventurous spirit and let her investigate the newest find. The remaining two women huddled around Liz, taking in the fresh, pine-scented aroma.

Kim's urgent voice erased any further thoughts of Christmas trees or the pine scent of burning candles. "Come… look what I've found!" called out Kim. When the other women found her, she was in a squatting position pointing to the fresh impression in the mud. Kim's eyes held an excited look as she asked, "What do you think it is… a bear?"

Barb, Sue and Liz gathered close to Kim to inspect her find. They all crouched low to the ground encircling the paw print. The sun peeked down among the female heads to shed some light for them to see. Sue placed her spread-out hand several centimetres above the print. She wanted to compare her hand size to the imprint left in the mud beside the creek. Her hand was much smaller. Sue's eyes met Barb and together they both said, "Black bear?" The five clawed toes and heel of the foot had made quite a deep impression in the mud, as well as on these women.

"Are... are you sure it's a black bear?" asked Kim.

"Well, I'm no expert, but I'm pretty sure," said Barb. She stood up to look about their surroundings and said, "I wonder which way he was travelling?"

The women joined the search and started looking for other tracks. Liz stepped across the creek by way of three large stones and started searching the other side for any sign of the powerful animal. Within minutes Liz spotted another track. "Here's one... it looks like he headed away from us!"

"Whew," said Kim, "I only like to read about bears, not meet them in person!" Sue noted that Kim's face now looked less stressed.

Barb had also seen the anxious expression disappear after Liz's announcement. Barb placed her arm around Kim's shoulder and said, "He's just filling up on berries, roots and nuts in preparation for denning throughout the winter." Barb continued the side-by-side hug to provide support to her friend. "He's long gone by now, Kim," she said with a smile. But Barb was not so sure... so she made a suggestion to the other women. "How about if we continue back on the trail... we can walk slowly and drink a cup of hot chocolate in our travel mugs." All the women agreed. Liz had returned from the other side of the creek... hopscotching off the last rock into the mud. She left a distinct size nine athletic shoe imprint, partially on top of the bear's print. "Oops," said Liz. "Sorry, I didn't mean to step on it."

"That's definitely encroachment on this animal's territory," said Kim, using a lawyer's tone of voice. They all smiled at their fun for a moment. But each woman knew just how fragile many endangered animals were in the wild. They could be destroyed as easily as the fractured paw print before them. It was a good reminder that this was the bear's territory and humans were the visitors here!

As they returned to the trail, Barb dug out her thermos and poured them all half-a-cup of steamy, hot chocolate. It was still early and the hot drink warmed their chilled bodies. They slowly continued their walk, following the trail west. Normally, the women were silent to avoid disturbing any bird or animal that they might encounter. But Barb had nearly twenty years of backpacking experience with Phillip and her sons and her nature sense told her that maybe they should make a bit of noise. After all, the black bear could have doubled back. There was no crunching of steps on dried leaves today and few birds to warn other animals of their presence. So, Barb started a conversation, "Black bears can be brown or cinnamon in colour… they're omnivores, which means bears will eat meat or vegetable. In the Fall, they especially like nuts because of their high fat content. Sometimes bears will eat for twenty hours a day in order to gain enough weight so they can hibernate for four to six months during the winter."

The women were now walking side-by-side along the path. It was a little snug, but felt good and allowed them to converse without any restrictions. "Rob told me that bears don't actually hibernate like rodents do," said Kim. "For Rob's birthday last month, I bought Wayne Lynch's 1993 book, *Bears — Monarchs of the Northern Wilderness.* Apparently they den to conserve energy during the cold winter and to get shelter where they can have their young." Kim took a hearty gulp of hot chocolate and continued, "Bears don't actually sleep for half a year… it's more like they're lethargic because their body temperature and heart rate drop. They don't eat, but they do give birth and who could sleep through that?" The women all chuckled at the thought.

"Sounds like a great way to lose weight," joked Liz and said, " I wonder if that's where the term *den mother* comes from?" Kim smiled and shrugged her shoulders, not knowing the answer. Liz continued with another question. "Does the male bear go in the den with his mate?"

Kim smiled, because she knew the answer to this question and responded. "Bears are mostly solitary animals and the only contact the female has with the male is during mating season... she is a continual single mother!"

Liz then asked, "How many cubs do they have, Kim?"

"Usually two or three cubs. She never leaves their side and will protect them from wolves and other bears, especially the male bears."

"Sounds like a typical mother to me," said Sue, "must be a lonely life in many ways though." Sue turned to face Barb. Their eyes met for several seconds and Barb read Sue's thoughts immediately.

"I don't like being single," said Barb, "but I'm glad I wasn't a young mother when I became a widow... that would be tough!"

Liz finished her chocolate drink and then commented, "I never really thought about being single. I certainly dated lots of men when I was younger and still do occasionally, but never found a man who was compatible with me. I'm quite content with my single status." Then she continued, "Sure, I get lonely sometimes, but that's why I have a great circle of friends."

"Perhaps that's where I went wrong," said Barb, "I depended on Phillip and his friends for companionship. Until you three came along, I had very few friends."

"So, is that what women should do?" asked Kim. "Build quality friendships to carry you through the good times and bad times, too?" The women all stopped walking and looked at Kim.

"You're one smart lady Kim, you know that," said Liz, smiling at her walking companion, "friends, yes, women need friends."

They had now walked several kilometres from where they had encountered the bear tracks. As the women walked west, they broke into a favourite African song. "Kum ba yah," had been sung by many young Canadian women around campfires and along the trails of the Rocky Mountains. As they climbed higher, the beauty of the forest was captivating. Somehow it was appropriate to sing this song whose African words meant "Come by here... my Lord," as the women walked together among the untouched beauty.

As the women got closer to the summit, they heard a faint roaring sound. At first, they thought it was just the wind, but with each step forward, they soon realized it was the distinct, refreshing sound of falling water. The trail took a long, sleepy turn to the right and as they walked on, the end of the path became brighter. Soon they focused on falling water right in front of them. The path literally ended at a sheer rock face, which looked out across a deep gorge. Directly across from where they stood was a spectacular water fall. It was not very wide, probably the width of a double garage door, but it started high above, off the cliff in front of them. It gushed over the edge and cascaded all the way down the granite slab into the gorge below. They could not see where the water landed, as the mist was too dense. Even though the powerful sound was deafening, the women stood for a long time breathing in the damp air and capturing the wonderful miracle with their other senses.

After some time had passed, the women decided to find a place where they could eat their lunches. They took a narrow dirt path, leading from the left side of the trail. There was a small clearing in the trees, where they had an excellent view of the waterfall in its entirety and it sheltered them from the powerful noise. They could also see the beginning of the river. It was almost noon when they broke into their day packs for their lunch. "What a perfect spot for lunch," said Liz, "it's breathtaking, as you promised Barb... thanks!"

As the women rested and took in some nourishment, Kim spotted a fat, Columbian ground squirrel, peeping out of a nearby hole in the ground. "Now there's one tubby squirrel that's really ready for his deep hibernation," said Kim, as she pointed at the brown-furred rodent.

"What's deep, hibernation Kim?" asked Liz.

"Well," said Kim, "rodents go into a dead sleep, whereas our friend, the bear, can be aroused." With that comment the ground squirrel disappeared back into his hole.

"I kind of like the idea of denning as bears do," said Liz, "I could finally get caught up on my reading and my sleep." Liz then placed her hands behind her head and slowly tipped over onto her back and looked up at the blue sky above. Barb and Kim smiled at the image of Liz all nestled into her urban den, piled high with books and pillows.

Sue, however, had been sitting very quietly and was not thinking about the same cozy images as her friends. It was only when Barb noticed the serious look on Sue's face that she asked her what was wrong. Sue heard Barb's voice and returned her thoughts to the present. "Oh, sorry, I was just thinking about the female bear." But Sue continued to look stressed. Barb made no further comment to her, but gently touched her arm. The silence continued to grow between them until Sue spoke. "Who in their right mind would want to be left alone with small children to look after? I'd be so afraid of being on my own!" Her words echoed across the gorge, breaking the sound of the constant falling water. Sue's voice sounded desperate and painful.

Liz quickly returned to a sitting position and said to Sue, "I didn't mean to upset you, Sue. You don't need to worry; you're married and have three great girls." Liz had spoken the words in kindness and sincerity to her friend. But Sue had already slipped further into her worried thoughts.

"Even if I were a bear in a den," Sue started, "I couldn't get any rest, I'd be too busy watching my cubs… I'd worry constantly about them!" Sue's voice now sounded shaky. Liz gently touched Sue on the other shoulder.

"You know, Sue," started Liz cautiously, "several weeks ago, you mentioned that women are sometimes like rag-dolls being pushed and pulled by everyone. I've been thinking about that statement ever since. Please tell me what you mean."

Sue focused her eyes on the grade five teacher and said, "It means, Liz, that everyone else is out of control and they are constantly wanting you to help them gain control. So I help them…. I… organize their lives, but they don't appreciate what I do for them!" Sue's hands flew up to her face to catch some of the tears that started to fall from her eyes. Kim now moved over to complete the circle of women around Sue. The women let Sue cry for several minutes, while they held her… it was a cleansing and spiritual moment for them all.

When Sue had finally stopped crying, she took several deep

breaths to calm herself. "Sorry, gals... I didn't mean to dump all those tears on you."

Liz smiled at Sue and said, "Well, we did come here to see waterfalls, we just didn't expect quite so many." Liz had a genuine smile on her face as she looked at Sue. Sue returned the smile and worked out a small giggle after Liz's comment.

Once Sue seemed more settled, Kim gently asked, "What I heard you say earlier, Sue, was that your sense of well-being is determined by other people's well-being. In other words," she asked, "are you living your life through your family? If they have a bad day... so do you?"

Sue looked directly at Kim and said, "Kim, I love my girls and I'd do for them what any mother would do... what's wrong with that?"

"Nothing," said Liz, "but just because your daughter is late for school, or fails a high school course, doesn't mean that you are a bad mother. It sounds to me like you want to control your family so that they won't disappoint you!" Sue just looked at Liz, she didn't know how to respond. Liz continued, "Failing and making mistakes is part of life and it's how we learn. Allowing people to make mistakes is a very growing experience." Liz looked from one woman to the other and then rested her eyes back on Sue. "I believe we're talking about co-dependency here!" said Liz.

Sue continued staring at Liz until Kim interrupted with a question. "What's co-dependency, again... I know I've read about it?"

Liz turned to Kim and answered, "It's when one lives her life through others. Like you said earlier, Kim, if a person is having a good day, then the co-dependent person will feel good and have a good day too." Kim nodded her head in response to the school teacher's answer and then Liz continued. "In some ways, we're all co-dependent because, as women and caregivers, our emotions are tied closely to others. We want and need to be empathetic to others, but we also need to be able to separate ourselves from them, so that we don't own their mistakes." The Fall wind gently blew Liz's words around each woman. All of them knew how easy it was to give and how difficult it was to know when to stop!

The sun continued to shine down on the four women seated near the waterfall. Sue and her hiking companions shifted their positions to become more comfortable... but all remained sitting close in support of Sue. Barb began with a comment about her sister's son. "My nephew is a recovering alcoholic and my sister had always blamed herself for his alcoholism. I would often hear her say, 'What did I do wrong? He attended Sunday school, sang in the church choir, was a good student.' I would tell her that she was no different than any other parent. You do the best you can, with what you know at the time. Your kids make choices, just like we do, some right, some wrong. It was *his* choice to drink every day... not my sister's. She used to fret constantly about this until she started going to Al-Anon, the support group for families of alcoholics. It really helped her deal with her co-dependency problem!"

Sue began shaking her head from side to side and then stated, "My girls aren't even old enough to drink and besides I don't have the problem... *they* do!"

Liz could see that Sue was missing the point, so commented further. "No one in your home has to be an alcoholic, for you to be co-dependent! It's just that many people who have co-dependent behaviours live or have lived with alcoholics."

Sue looked and sounded very frustrated when she continued, "They don't appreciate what I do for them." Sue began to sob again. "I worry about the silliest things... sometimes I seem to be preoccupied with their behaviour. Like when Dawn started gaining weight last summer. I became obsessed with everything she put in her mouth. I would search her room for junk food and feel so bad if I found any chocolate bar wrappers." Sue blew her nose and continued, "Last week Brian came home smelling of alcohol, so I've been calling him at the office all week to see if he's there or out at the bar. Sometimes it makes me crazy... is this... co-dependency?" Sue's eyes were puffy from crying and her voice had a pleading tone for help.

As all the women nodded their heads in one affirming motion,

Barb glanced up and noticed a large coloured arc that had formed above the mist from the waterfall. "Look," she said and pointed at the rainbow. The women all turned to see how the reflected bundle of sunrays had created a brilliant rainbow in front of their waterfall. Each misty drop acted as a tiny prism, splitting the sunrays into their component colours. This image of the sun's reflection was a collection of multiple colours, from deep violet to soft yellow. Barb was now right behind Sue and placed her hands firmly on both her shoulders. The women were mesmerized by the richness of the colours. Even the gentle wind, that had followed them on their journey, had stopped to take a long look at the spectacular event.

Several minutes had passed without any words being spoken. The women all sensed such peace and tranquillity, especially Sue. Taking a long, slow breath, Sue said, "This is what I need to find in my life... some peace." Barb gave Sue's shoulders a firm squeeze to affirm her comment.

Liz smiled at Sue and then said, "Accepting that there are things in your life you can change and things that you cannot change, will help bring you the peace you seek, Sue." Sue returned the smile to Liz.

Then Barb gently turned Sue with her hands, so that she faced her. "Perhaps if you could let go... and let God?" said Barb. As Sue heard these words, she thought that Barb's face was that of an angel... filled with love. "Letting go of other people's lives may be a turning point in your life," said Barb, "and accepting others for who they are and allowing them to make their own choices will set you free from your pain."

The colourful arc remained tethered to the waterfall for several hours. Sue and the other women continued to enjoy the serenity of the forest and afternoon sun. It was nearly 3:00 p.m. before they decided to gather their things and start the long trail back to the birch grove. They walked in silence, not concerned about bears, but wanting to continue the peaceful feeling that each woman had found at the waterfall. Sue had been strengthened by the love of her friends and the fresh insight into her co-dependency behaviours. "Yes," she thought to herself, "I want to learn more and try to understand why I feel the way I do about the people I love. Tomorrow," thought Sue, feeling a sense of true happiness for the first time in weeks, "I'll go to the library and borrow some books that will help me understand co-dependency."

Over halfway down the trail, Sue broke the silence by starting to sing… "Kum ba yah, my Lord, Kum ba yah." And soon three female voices joined in harmony with Sue's. The forest was no longer silent, but it was filled with peace as the women walked back to the birch grove.

SERENITY PRAYER

*God grant me
the serenity to
accept the things
I cannot change,
the courage to change
the things I can,
and the wisdom
to know the
difference.*

Amen

CHAPTER SIX

The renal dialysis unit where Barb worked had been busy all day. She was glad to see the hands of the clock reach 4:30 p.m., so she could relinquish the duties to a fresh Registered Nurse. Work on the unit was not only physically tiring, but emotionally draining as well. Apart from the various tasks and procedures, Barb had to try and instill hope in each one of her clients. For without donor kidneys, their lives would be forever tied, literally, to these dialysis machines.

As Barb finished writing her last nursing note about one of her clients, she focused on the date she wrote… October 28th. A dark shadow tugged deeply at her heart. She then paused momentarily in memory of her parents. Five years ago today, her mother and father had been in a fatal car accident. They were going on holiday to the east coast of Canada to tour the Atlantic provinces. She recalled the last time she saw her parents. Barb, Phillip and the boys had invited them over for dinner. It was a great evening with laughter and sharing some personal moments that Barb would treasure forever. Then two days later, the R.C.M.P. had called with the terrible news. A semi-trailer truck had crossed over the centre line of the highway… they were gone. Barb swallowed hard remembering the pain and loss she felt at that moment.

Then, suddenly, a warm supportive hand gently grasped her

shoulder. It belonged to Lois, her nursing supervisor. She looked down at Barb, smiled and said, "It's time to go home."

The tactile exchange had helped Barb gain some self control over her thoughts and when returning the smile to Lois, she said, "Thanks, I was just finishing up."

Barb had transferred to this unit after Phillip died. She had wanted to work part-time and this was the only position available. But the move turned out to be a positive one, for her supervisor was a fair and consistent manager. Barb always knew day-in and day-out what to expect from her. They were a good match.

It was beginning to get dark when Barb left the hospital and walked the eight blocks to her home. The fresh Fall air felt good. She smiled, knowing that tomorrow was Wednesday, a day which gave her such peace and joy... and fun with her forest friends. But tomorrow was the last day the women would meet, as the weather was getting far too cold in the foothills. Barb sighed, thinking about how she was going to miss these outings. They always seemed to learn so much from each other... it was stimulating and growthful. As Barb continued her walk home, a cool north wind followed in her footsteps.

At the same time across the city, Kim was sitting at the stop light on Sixteenth Avenue, waiting for the light to turn green. She looked forward to picking Kyle up from the babysitter. He was such a delightful little boy and she could hardly wait to give him a big hug. Just then, her cellular phone rang, making her jump! It was Rob, her husband, "I just got home and there was a letter from my parents." There was a long pause before Rob continued. "They're thinking of leaving Hong Kong after Christmas and coming here. They... they... want to move in with us." Rob listened carefully, but heard no response from his wife. All he could hear was the sound of his own heart pumping, so he continued, "I mean, it's not for sure. Just because it's the Chinese custom, doesn't mean it has to happen." More silence. "Kim, Kim, are you there?" asked Rob, in a slightly panicky voice.

"Yes, yes, I'm here... I just don't know what to say. I mean, I guess... I thought that there would always be just the three of us, hum... " Kim was at a loss for words. This had taken her completely by surprise. As the light turned green, she commented to Rob, "Honey, I have to go, the light just changed, I'll pick Kyle up and be home in twenty minutes." Rob never got a chance to say goodbye before she hung up.

Sue was cleaning up the dinner dishes with Brian's help. She heard the phone ring and then the familiar yell, "I got it," from her daughter Dawn. Sue and Brian gave a tired smile to each other, wondering if they could survive through their three daughters' teenage years. Several minutes later, Dawn hurried into the kitchen with the cordless phone and said, "It's for you Mom. It's grandma and could you please get the other line if it rings. I'm expecting a call from Jason." Before Sue could answer her youngest daughter, she disappeared into the nearest bathroom.

"I'll finish up the dishes," said Brian, "you go visit with your mother."

"Thanks," said Sue, giving Brian a quick kiss on his cheek.

She went into the front room, away from the noisy dishwasher and the loud pop-rock music that was playing from three separate bedrooms. "Hi, Mom... sorry, I was finishing the dishes. How are you?"

"Oh, I've been better. My back has been so painful since Sunday... I wondered if you could take me to the doctor's tomorrow morning?"

"Tomorrow," answered Sue, "tomorrow is Wednesday Mom, I go for my hike with my friends in the forest. Can't Theresa take you?"

"You know that your sister doesn't know how to handle me the way you do dear and I get so nervous when she drives me in that old beat-up car. It's not safe!"

"Mom, please," continued Sue, "I can't take you tomorrow. It's our last hike of the year and I'm driving." Sue's mother was silent. So, Sue continued, "Why don't you have Theresa drop you off at the doctor's office and take a cab home when you're done?"

Sue's mother continued her attack, "Doesn't Theresa work day shift at the bank tomorrow, Sue?"

"No Mom, she always works 4:00 p.m. to 8:00 p.m., on Wednesdays."

"Oh," said the exasperated septuagenarian.

"Why don't you call her and ask her to take you?" said Sue.

"Oh, I hate to bug her around the supper hour. Will you call Theresa and arrange it for me? I'm really tired!"

Sue took a deep breath and let it out slowly. "It was supper hour here too!" thought Sue. She had been reading quite a bit about co-dependency lately and was working hard to conquer the word NO. The silence was interrupted by her mother's voice again asking her to call her sister for her. "No, Mom, you call her yourself," said a confident Sue, as the other line beeped in her right ear.

"All right, all right," said Sue's mother, "ask one little favour of your oldest daughter and . . ."

Sue cut her mother's sentence off by saying, "Let's not go here, Mom," using a current phrase of her daughter, when she didn't want to talk about an issue. "I'll call you tomorrow night when I get home," said Sue, trying to finish the conversation. Another beep sounded on the phone as she completed her last sentence. Her mother was about to start another round of arguing, but Sue cut her off again, saying there was someone on the other line and she had to go! As soon as Sue said "Goodbye," her finger touched the receiver button to retrieve the other caller. "Hello, hello," said Sue, as her ears strained to hear another voice, but the line was blank.

Dawn had suddenly appeared beside her, "Is it for me?" she asked, in an excited voice.

Turning to her daughter she said, "No, no, I must have just missed them."

Dawn's face looked like a volcano about to explode. "Mom, I told you to get the other line… I was expecting another call!"

Sue was about to explain how her mother was not aware they had two lines on their phone, but Dawn already had a "mad-on," snatched the phone from her mother and stomped off to her bedroom. Sue stood there, realizing that the only buttons being pushed tonight were her own. "This is not an easy time in my life," thought Sue, "I'm trying to meet the needs of my mother and my daughters. And I'm caught right in the middle!"

Sue returned to the kitchen to find Brian finishing up the last of the dishes. "Thanks," she said giving a warm smile to her husband. He smiled back and extended his arms to give her a much needed hug. They stood in the kitchen for a long time, holding onto each other during the rinse cycle of the dishwasher.

"What *am* I going to do?" thought Liz, as she glanced through several pamphlets on health care resources. Liz already had the Victorian Order of Nurses coming in every day to help get her mother up and make sure she had breakfast and lunch. But her mother's physical condition continued to deteriorate and Liz was having trouble meeting her mother's remaining needs. Liz had several volunteers driving her mother to physical therapy and doctor appointments throughout the day, but it was the evenings that were becoming more difficult for Liz to handle. Liz's mother, Florence, required assistance in the bathroom, getting to bed and also needed help to be turned in bed during the night. Liz really didn't mind helping her mother because she truly loved her. But Liz wanted to start taking some evening classes to work on her Master's degree. She also wanted to provide more self-care to herself. Her weekly hikes with her friends were just the beginning of her self- nourishment program. Florence simply needed too much help to be left alone in the evening... and then there was that incident last Friday night!

Liz's week had been very busy at school. Friday night she slept like a log, only to be wakened by her mother crying. When she dashed into her mother's room, she found Florence sobbing, "I called and called, but you didn't come... I needed to go to the bathroom." Florence tried to catch her breath before she continued, "I... I... had an accident in my bed!"

"Oh, Mom, I'm so sorry... I didn't hear you," was the only response that Liz could make.

At that point, Liz realized that her mother's care was becoming a full-time job. As Liz glanced through the last pamphlet on long-term care facilities, she recalled what Florence had said clearly to her on the subject. "I want to stay in my own home… what's wrong with that?"

"Nothing… everything," thought Liz.

Just then, Liz heard the familiar voice calling out, "Elizabeth, I'm ready to be put to bed… are you there, dear?"

"I'll be right there, Mom," answered Liz, from her den down the hall. Liz turned the desk light off and walked out of the darkened room to attend to her mother.

The cool, dark night seemed to pass much too quickly for the women of the forest. When radio alarms turned on the next morning, there was a moment when they all wished that they could have just a few… more minutes of sleep. But as each woman slowly woke up, she became energized with the thought of a new adventure… and sharing it with her friends.

Sue had offered to drive them all out in her mini-van. It was still early, so they decided to have a hot drink at the coffee shop before taking the drive west. There had been a light skiff of snow overnight, but there were no clouds in the sky that morning and the sun looked like it was going to shine.

It was nearly 9:30 a.m. when they arrived at the birch grove. As each woman stepped out of the van, the chilly air stung at their exposed flesh. "Oh," said Liz, "it's mighty fresh out here!" The women wore wool hats, mitts and extra sweaters under their jackets. A light covering of snow was just enough to cover all the brown bushes and barren ground. The birch grove had a new, clean look about it. Soon all the women were ready for their final hike of the season.

"Today's hike," started Barb, "is going to be a surprise. It's a fairly short walk… about an hour and a half directly west." Each of the women slowly smiled at Barb, wondering what could possibly await them.

Liz looked directly at Barb and asked, "Any hills in our travels, perchance?" A round of giggling from all the women broke the silent,

Fall air.

Partly through her last chuckle, Barb responded, "Not today, Liz!"

"Whew," came a sound directly from Liz.

Sue then commented, "Sounds like you're almost ready to pack it in for the season, Liz?"

"Oh, not really. I haven't been sleeping as well lately and report cards are due next week." With that statement, Liz expelled a large volume of warm air from her lungs, creating a misty cloud in front of her. It seemed to float there, frozen for several seconds, then suddenly it dissipated right before the women's eyes.

Sue smiled at Liz, grabbed her by the hand and said, "Come on, partner, let's get this hike underway so we can warm up."

As the women followed Barb into the forest, their footprints left impressions in the light snow. When they started their walk, they didn't see or hear anything except their own breath and footsteps. It seemed as if they were the only creatures in the forest today.

After walking along the path for some time, a small clearing appeared on the left side of the trail. The women of the forest decided that this was a good place to have a hot drink and take a closer look at the small trees, known as blue elders. While Kim, Liz and Barb dug out the thermos and cups, Sue walked over to inspect a short, trunked tree. The elders were more like a shrub than a tree, as they were only about three metres high. Sue stood beside one of the many low branches and stared at the snowflakes, which had taken refuge there over the night. Each snowflake was a unique and fragile piece of nature. "Imagine," thought Sue, "these snowflakes together in community... create snow!" Sue took a deep breath and gently blew near the branch, scattering the tiny flakes into the fresh, morning air. They sparkled as the sun filtered through each one.

Barb had arrived quietly carrying two steamy mugs in hand. She had watched Sue's inspection of the snow flakes and thought, "What a gentle spirit Sue has." Barb remained quiet, not wanting to spoil this moment. But the smell of sweet apple cider had reached Sue's nostrils and lifted her from the dream state. As Sue sipped the warm, golden mixture, she asked Barb, "Are these blue elders?"

Barb nodded her head in response to Sue's question. She gently touched the scaly bark and said, "Their wood has no commercial value, but their berries are used for making terrific jam, jellies and pie."

"And wine, too!" said Liz, as she joined in. "My mother and dad had an elder tree in their back yard. They made wine every Fall from the bluish-black berries." Liz took a sip of her apple cider and then continued, "I remember my dad telling me that the roots, stems and leaves are toxic. The native Canadians used their emetic and purgative properties when one of their tribe ate something bad." Both Sue and Barb had made mental notes of this information.

"I also recall," added Barb, "they're not a very strong tree... they need protection from the wind. That's why they grow near the centre of the forest."

Kim had now joined the huddle of women near the trail. "Did I hear you say that these trees are called blue elders?" The other three women all nodded their heads, affirming the answer. "Hum," said Kim, "are they named after older people?" In answer to Kim's question the other women held surprised looks on their faces.

But Barb shook away the startled expression first saying, "What makes you say that Kim?"

"Oh, I just wondered... because in some ways, they kind of remind me of older adults." There was a pause in the conversation as the women thought about Kim's comment.

"Perhaps she is right," thought Sue, "my mother, like these shrubs, is a small, fragile woman, who does get down or blue at times. I know she gets lonely... and annoyed... when I can't spend as much time with her as I'd like."

Barb remembered her mother, who used to spend a lot of time playing bridge with her friends. "Older people often live separate from their families," thought Barb. "These blue elders live by themselves, too, just off the trail. They can watch the comings and goings of all the hikers who pass by." Barb recalled the time she had worked on a geriatric unit at the hospital. Many of the seniors sat around the nursing station, just to watch and perhaps to be near other people.

Liz remembered Barb commenting about how blue elders were not very strong and needed protection. "That's my mom all right," thought Liz, "she needs me to help take care of her."

As the women continued with their private thoughts, the blue elders delighted in having company. There had not been anyone by their way all month. They tried to straighten their bent and crooked branches, in hopes that they would look more appealing to their visitors. Perhaps they would spend the day with them.

Soon the women continued their conversation. "That's an interesting analogy, Kim," said Barb, "what made you think of it?"

Kim continued, "Well it's just that I've had Rob's parents on my mind since yesterday. They sent us a letter, asking if they could move in with us."

"Really," said Barb, "are you going to... ." But when Barb looked at Kim's face, the answer was obvious. "Oh, I can see you're not too pleased about the idea," said Barb.

"Well actually, Barb, it's just I haven't had time to think it through. You see in the Chinese culture, when the son's parents become old, it's common for them to move in with their son's family. Perhaps I've adapted to the Canadian way, where the nuclear families live alone and place their parents in care facilities."

Liz swallowed the last few drops of the now cool apple cider. She thought about Kim's words very carefully before she spoke. "Most adult children take very good care of their parents, Kim... we only place them in care facilities if we are unable to care for them ourselves."

Kim smiled back at Liz, knowing that Liz was doing all that she could for her mother. "I know," said Kim, "It's just that I thought there would always be the three of us. I know that many Chinese are leaving Hong Kong. It's home to Rob's parents... I just thought they would always stay there."

Sue had listened carefully to Kim's situation and added a comment, "Sometimes our lives turn out differently than we plan!"

Sue's words had spoken the truth. There was a comfortable silence among the women as each thought about how her life had taken different turns. Soon they were on their way again. They walked down the trail, leaving the blue elders without saying goodbye.

The women continued their hike west for another twenty minutes. When they came to a fork in the trail, Barb led them to the right. Within a few more minutes, they heard the sound of running water. Beside them was a wide, slow-moving stream, which they followed for another ten minutes. Mountain-ash, willows and white elm trees grew in this part of the forest. They were all good sized trees, that needed to live near the water. Barb suddenly stopped and pointed through the trees. It was a little difficult to make out, but up ahead, through the trees, was a small lake. "Where are we?" asked Kim.

All of the women looked to Barb for the answer. Barb had a huge grin on her face when she answered the question. "We're at the centre of the forest. Just up ahead, in the middle of the back-water from this stream, is a large beaver lodge."

"Beavers.... are we going to see some beavers?" asked an excited Kim.

"Yup," said Barb, "but be really quiet now... and follow me." Barb lead the women off the trail toward a higher ridge, overlooking the stream. The women slowly worked their way up through fallen trees and thick bushes. Liz was so excited that she almost passed Barb, hurrying to reach the ridge. Once at the top, the view was spectacular. To the left, was the stream that they had followed earlier. The dam was as long as a city block and the back-water was deep blue in colour. Directly in front of them, in the centre of the back-water, was a miniature mountain of mud, sticks, logs and debris... the beaver lodge. The women were hidden in a natural blind of fallen logs and small bushes. It was a perfect spot. The sun was warmer now and the challenging climb to the ridge had heated their bodies. So, they decided to just sit and watch in hopes of seeing the large, reddish brown rodent.

The morning had turned out to be perfect... it was a clear, calm day. The women whispered back and forth among each other about everything they saw and heard. Liz spotted the first beaver swimming toward the lodge with several twigs in his mouth. "He looks like a powerful swimmer," commented Liz, "I wonder how much he weighs?"

"Hum, that's hard to say," said Barb, "but most adults weigh between fifteen and forty kilograms... big enough!" They watched the rodent, Canada's national emblem, waddle part way on top of the lodge and jam the sticks he was carrying into the structure.

"Looks like he's repairing the lodge for winter," said Sue and then she asked, "say, Barb, do they hibernate like the other rodents?"

Barb lowered her voice so as not to be heard by the beavers and answered the question. "No, they don't hibernate... they're too busy looking after their family."

"What do you mean?" asked Sue.

"Beavers normally mate for life," answered Barb. "Each lodge contains the adult pair, newborn kits and yearlings born from the previous year. They're busy little beavers!" The women all giggled with that remark. Barb soon continued, "Naturally they do sleep more in the winter and when they get hungry, they swim deep under the lodge and pull up bark and twigs from their food stash."

Just then, several smaller beavers appeared from under the water. "Hey, where did they come from?" asked Kim.

Liz knew the answer to this question from teaching her grade five students a unit on beavers. "Their front door is under water, Kim," said Liz, "it's how they protect themselves from predators." The sun continued to warm the Fall air, as the women sat watching the lodge of the busy beavers.

It was now almost 12:30 p.m. and time to eat their packed lunches. Liz had brought a blanket for them all to sit on, as the ground was much too cold. They sat huddled together, taking in some healthy nourishment. Sue poured some steamy, Irish cream coffee out of a large thermos for all of the women. "Oh Sue, that smells so good," said Liz. Then, after taking a sip, Liz commented further, "and tastes even better."

"Thanks," said Sue, "It's one of my favourites."

As Kim held a warm mug between her hands she said, "I wonder if the beavers are having their lunch too?"

"Perhaps they are," responded Barb, "they pretty much do everything as a family unit. Sometimes there can be as many as twelve beavers living in a lodge."

"Wow," exclaimed Kim, "sounds like the Chinese!" Smiles appeared on everyone's face, except for Liz. "What wrong Liz?" asked Kim.

Liz held a sad expression on her face, then gave a half smile and said, "Oh, nothing really, I guess I was just wishing that I could have had some brothers or sisters, so that they could help me take care of my mother."

"You're doing a great job with your mother, Liz," said Barb, in a very caring tone. "I'm very proud of you. I only wish I still had my parents here... I know I'd do anything for them, too."

Liz placed her arm around Barb, nodded her head and said, "Thanks... I do want to continue to help my mother, but I need to care for *me* sometimes, too. I've been so tired lately. Do you think I'm being too selfish?"

"I know how you're feeling Liz," said Sue, in an anxious voice, "I'm living proof of the sandwich generation. I'm caught in the middle between the needs of my mother and the needs of my girls. And what about my needs... and your needs," pointing at Liz. "We're not being selfish, we've given all our lives and we can still give, but now we also need to nourish ourselves!"

They heard the splash of beaver tails, realizing that their voices were disturbing their neighbours. Sue continued, "I'm slowly learning that I can't do it all... that's why there are support groups and resource centres! They provide information to help adult children manage older adult care concerns." Sue looked over at Kim and asked, "What are you going to do about Rob's parents?"

"Like I said earlier, Sue, I really don't know... but I do need some time to weigh out all the options. I mean, if they moved in, I would have an instant babysitter for Kyle. It also means that I will likely become the second woman of the house... Rob's mother would always be first... that's tradition."

"Oh," responded Sue, in a lowered voice. "How do you feel about that?" Kim sat up straighter and looked toward the beaver lodge before she answered the question. "I remember mentioning to you before that our culture values old people. We see living together as a positive option. People learn to truly share... to give and take. In fact, it may be a very growthful environment for our son to be raised in." Kim swallowed the last of her coffee, then finished her sentence. "Like I said, I will weigh all the advantages and disadvantages of them moving in. Rob's parents are very open people and have always treated me very well. It could work if we can be open and express all our feelings."

Barb smiled at Kim and said, "I know you will do what is best for you, Rob, Kyle and your in-laws."

Smiling back at Barb's tawny-skinned face, Kim said, "Thanks for your vote of confidence!"

The women had been sitting for over an hour and needed to shift positions on the blanket. From the beaver lodge, the large rodent noticed hands and arms stretching skyward... it was an odd sight. Kim continued to watch the beaver lodge and reported any activity to the others. Liz had perched herself on an old log to help catch some of the sun's warm rays. And the other two women put all of their garbage into one day pack, to be carried out later.

Sue thought about what Liz had said earlier... referring to the fact that she had no siblings to help care for her mother. She decided to share something with Liz and the others. "You know Liz, my sister is quite capable of doing all kinds of things for my mother, but it's my mother that would rather have me do it. I hadn't thought of it before now, but I think it's her way of giving me a compliment!"

"But at least you have a sister to ask," said Liz. "Sometimes care giving feels like such a heavy responsibility... other times, it's such a joy!"

Sue reached out and squeezed Liz's right hand. "I hear you friend," said Sue, "welcome to motherhood!"

Liz gave a slight smile before she continued, "My mother was a professional wife and mother. She never worked outside the home. She also never made many friends or joined a women's group. She was always there for me, though." Liz's words had a guilty tone to them.

After Liz had spoken, she looked out toward the beaver lodge. For the first time that day, she focused on what lay beyond it. "Hey, I didn't notice that before!"

"What?" asked the observant Kim, always eager to find something new.

Liz continued, "Over there, on the other side of the back-water, just beyond that first meadow. There must have been a forest fire a few years ago!" All of the women stood up, startling three little beavers. They dove under the water for protection.

"You're right Liz," said Barb, "I remember this happened over five years ago. We brought my parents up here for a hike and had a picnic lunch among the lodge-pole pines. My mother said she had never seen such a beautiful spot. The following week, the park rangers had to close off this area because of the fire."

"What are lodge-pole pines?" questioned Kim.

Barb pointed to the far right... "Those are lodge-pole pines. See how tall and straight they are! Native Canadians used them to build teepees." Barb placed the fingertips of both her hands together, making the shape of the teepee. She then continued, "What is so remarkable about the lodge-pole pine is that it's a tree reborn from fire!"

"What do you mean?" inquired Kim.

"You see, Kim," said Barb, "pine cones hold one tough little seed. In fact, the seeds will only pop out of the cone at forty degrees centigrade."

"The fire?" questioned, Kim.

"Yes, Kim, the fire destroys the mature trees, but the seeds fall onto fertile ground. Those metre-high trees over there are a result of that devastating fire five years ago." Barb stared at the young trees, but thought about a picnic she had shared with her husband and parents... now gone. Barb drew in a breath of fresh air. She could feel it revitalize her spirit. As she exhaled the stale air, it also removed some of the painful memories from her mind. The women also took advantage of the peaceful moment. They thought about how fortunate they were to live in such a wonderful country, with good families and friends.

Kim had become a wonderful student of Mother Nature. She had listened and learned a great deal over the past few months. As Kim took in a breath of the clean, fresh air, she made a profound comment. "So, out of disaster... comes life. Out of bad... comes good!"

Barb turned her head toward Kim and softly spoke, "Out of the death of those trees comes life and such wonderful memories of Phillip, my parents and... all of you!" As Barb's wonderful gift touched each woman... tears filled their eyes.

"You know," said Kim, "maybe having Rob's parents move in with us might be a really good thing."

"Sounds to me like we're talking about serendipity!" said Sue and then continued. "Because of my mother's osteoporosis, I work harder on taking care of myself and eating a diet rich in calcium sources. I'm also learning that I can't do everything. I'm learning to say NO, even to my mother!"

"Hum, serendipity," said Liz, "out of bad things... good things come along." Liz thought silently for several more minutes and, because the women were comfortable with silence, they just let its magic work among friends. When Liz started to speak, it was as though she was waking up from a long sleep. Her words were slow and her voice was deep. "I've been worrying so much about my mother lately. I'm concerned that I can't care for all her needs."

Sue gently touched Liz's hand and said, "There are resources out there who can help you, Liz."

"I know, Sue, but I feel guilty when I think about my needs first. Yet, I also know that hanging onto guilt can scar the remainder of my life. It's something that I'm going to have to let go!" The women all nodded their heads, knowing how guilt can rob the human spirit of energy and peace. "I'm trying to do the best I can for her and for me. I think living apart would be hard on us both... we've always been together." Liz smiled at her female companions who had come to know her so well. "Perhaps I should talk to her about both our fears. What is it that you said earlier, Sue? Sometimes life takes a turn we didn't expect? My mother didn't expect to get arthritis. I didn't expect at age fifty-one to feel the need for self-care!"

The family of beavers came out of their lodge one more time before the women had to leave. "We're just like them," said Sue, "always busy doing something."

"Yes," said Liz, as she gave a side-to-side hug with Sue. "As long as you're busy doing something you enjoy, then when you're tired... it's a good tired!"

Kim joined Sue at her other side and said, "When I'm at the end of my life, I want to look back and say that it was great... no regrets!"

Sue turned to Kim and responded, "That's why we're always working to improve ourselves... to have a quality life!"

The women didn't want to leave the forest, but it was almost 3:00 p.m. As Liz looked back, she saw the reflection of the beaver lodge in the still, blue water. This centre had come to symbolize caring for each other and for themselves. The hike back to the birch grove seemed to happen too fast. This time they did stop at the blue elders to say goodbye. Yes, they were small, fragile little shrubs, but these women had become their friends. The women of the forest cared very deeply for one another, their families and the forest. The blue elders were glad to have met them on this day. As the afternoon sun touched each branch, the elders held their branches high. Yes, they were nothing like some of the other trees, but they were proud to belong in the forest, near its centre... the centre of caring.

"To everything there is a season and a time to every purpose under the heaven... a time to heal; a time to break down and a time to build up... a time to weep and a time to laugh."

Ecclesiastes 3 : 1-4

ABOUT THE AUTHOR

Photovisions — Calgary

LINDA J. ORMSON

Linda is a native Calgarian, who graduated from Sheridan College School of Nursing in Oakville, Ontario, in 1982. As a Registered Nurse, her interest and experience has been working as an advocate for older adults. Besides providing workshops on positive aging issues in the Calgary area, you will often find Linda on TV, radio, or in the newspaper speaking for and about seniors. She writes and publishes articles, short stories and helpful handouts on positive aging issues to families of older adults. Linda is the author/publisher of her 1989 book, SOCKS... and other warm thoughts... a positive poetry-story on mid-life aging.

Linda is also completing a Bachelor of Nursing Degree at Athabasca University. She volunteers on various committees for older adults, her local community and church. Linda currently is the Coordinator of the Victorian Order of Nurses, Home Sharing Program. This program helps keep older adults living in their own home, by matching younger people to live with them who will help the senior. Linda was honoured in 1992 as a nominee for the YWCA, Women of Distinction Awards, in the Health and Well-being category. She enjoys playing golf and is a marathon swimmer. And finally, as a women challenged with arthritis since 1977, she believes that knowledge is the key to empowerment. In her words, "We all have disabilities, whether you are poor at math, wear glasses or use a cane to help you walk. Everyone has areas that challenge us daily. The goal is to accept your limitations and go with *gusto* on your abilities! Believe in yourself. Love yourself for who you are and what special gifts you bring to others."

ABOUT THE EDITOR

MAUREEN McMANUS

Maureen was born and formally educated in south-east England. In 1966, she emigrated to Montreal from Switzerland, where she worked for the World Health Organization in Geneva. After an uninspiring move to Ottawa and a subsequent marriage break-up, Maureen relocated to Calgary in 1984 with a computer software company. Between 1986 and 1994, she raised funds for Operation Eyesight Universal (OEU), first as a volunteer and then as a staff member. As a result, she travelled through India three times and her work also took her to African countries. Since being "restructured" out of OEU in 1994, Maureen has enjoyed pastimes dear to her heart, such as horseback riding; hanging around Spruce Meadows equestrian centre; volunteering for a therapeutic riding program and for Rotary; playing tennis; snowshoeing; cross-country skiing; arts activities; as well as her skin care and colour cosmetics consulting business. However, Maureen's major pastime has been the pursuit of a Bachelor of Arts Degree through the Distance Education Program of the University of Waterloo — writing term papers has been great experience for becoming an editor! To help finance her favourite activities, Maureen has worked on contract as a fundraiser for a Calgary hospital foundation. Maureen loves to travel and explore new places, but is always happy to come back to Alberta, where she can marvel at the grandeur of Mother Nature and Her variety of magical, mystical horses. Starting in May, 1996, Maureen will be working with the High River District Health Care Foundation.

ABOUT THE COVER DESIGN ARTIST

Photovisions — Calgary

BRAD HENDRICKS

Brad is a native Calgarian, whose talent for drawing started during his high school years. Brad is moving into his third year of studies at Alberta College of Art and Design. He enjoys playing hockey and camping during the summer months. Brad looks forward to a career in advertising / or graphic design.

REFERENCE LIST

Atlas of Canada. (1981). Montreal: Reader's Digest.

Beattie, Melody. (1987). <u>Codependent no more.</u> Centre City, MN: Hazeldon Educational Materials.

Byers, Andrew. (Ed.) (1991). <u>Canadian book of the road.</u> (3rd ed.). Montreal: Readers Digest Canada.

Cassidy, J., Scheffel, R. (Eds.) (1990). <u>Book of North American birds.</u> New York: Readers Digest.

Hosie, R.C. (1979). <u>Native trees of Canada.</u> (8th ed.). Don Mills, Ont: Fitzhenry & Whiteside, Canadian Forestry & Canadian Government.

Kroll, Ken., & Levy Klein, Erica. (1992). <u>Enabling romance: a guide to love, sex and relationships for the disabled (and the people who care about them).</u> New York: Harmony Books.

Lynch, Wayne. (1993). <u>Bears — monarchs of the northern wilderness.</u> Vancouver: Greystone Books.

Marsh, James H. (Ed.) . (1985). <u>The Canadian Encyclopedia.</u> (Vols. 1-3). Edmonton: Hurtig Publishers.

McDonnell, K., & Valverde, M. (Eds.) . (1991). <u>The healthsharing book: resources for Canadian women.</u> Toronto: Women's Press

Novak, Mark. (1993). <u>Aging & society: a Canadian perspective.</u> (2nd ed.) Scarborough: Nelson Canada.

Sheehy, Gail. (1984). <u>Passages.</u> New York: Bantam Books.

<u>The new our bodies ourselves.</u> (1984). New York: The Boston's Women's Health Collective & Simon & Schuster Inc.

Whitney, E., & Hamilton, E., & Rolfes, S. (1990). <u>Understanding nutrition.</u> (5th ed.) . St. Paul, MN: West Publishing.